THE MASTER OF MONKTON MANOR

Homeless, Megan Clegg is forced to take up a position as lady's maid in Manor House, the home of Lady Mary Jarvis and her son, Samuel, who runs the estate. But soon Megan begins to suspect that behind the manor's dignified exterior something sinister is going on. It is only when a young boy is found dead on the rocks below the cliffs, and murder is suspected, that the truth finally comes to light — and it is then that Megan finds love . . .

HOME IS WHERE THE HEART IS

Mavis Thomas

Venetia had loved her husband dearly. Now she and their small daughter were living alone in a beautiful, empty home. Seeking fresh horizons in a Northern seaside town, Venetia finds deep interest in work with a Day Centre for the Elderly — and two very different men. If ever she could rediscover love, would Terry bring it with his caring, healing laughter? Or would it be Jay, the once well-known singer now at the final crossroads of his troubled career?

HEART UNDER SIEGE

Joy St Clair

Gemma had no interest in men — which was how she had acquired the job of companion/secretary to Mrs Prescott in Kentucky. The old lady had stipulated that she wanted someone who would not want to rush off and get married. But why was the infuriating Shade Lambert so sceptical about it? Gemma was determined to prove to him that she meant what she said about remaining single — but all she proved was that she was far from immune to his devastating attraction!

VALERIE HOLMES

---◆---

THE MASTER OF MONKTON MANOR

Complete and Unabridged

LINFORD
Leicester

First published in Great Britain in 2002

First Linford Edition
published 2003

British Library CIP Data

Holmes, Valerie
  The master of Monkton Manor.
  —Large print ed.—
  Linford romance library
  1. Love stories
  2. Large type books
  I. Title
  823.9'2 [F]

ISBN 1–8439–5050–2

Published by
F. A. Thorpe (Publishing)
Anstey, Leicestershire

Set by Words & Graphics Ltd.
Anstey, Leicestershire
Printed and bound in Great Britain by
T. J. International Ltd., Padstow, Cornwall

This book is printed on acid-free paper

1

Fetcher sat on the hard, wooden seat by the open fire of the inn. Its tall, unyielding back seemed to emphasise his slight frame as he sat patiently, chewing the end of his long, clay pipe.

'They should've been here by now, Fetcher, shouldn't they?' Jack asked nervously from where he sat on the stone surround of the low window.

He was fifteen and impatient by nature. His job was to watch through the gap between the shutters for the flicker of a lantern from out at sea. His eyes needed to be young, astute and keen, especially on a winter's night such as this.

'You keep yer mind and eyes on yer job, lad. They'll come, they always do,' Fetcher answered in a calm voice, then emptied his pewter tankard of ale in one large last gulp and set it back down on the upturned barrel, which served as his table.

Fetcher stared at the recumbent figure of Amos Barton, the licensee of the Coble Inn in the sandy hamlet of Seaham. He was a large, rosy-cheeked man with a well-fed stomach and an apparently jovial air about him, but those who knew him were not fooled by the appearance of the lazy landlord or his pleasant, affable manner. He was as strong as an ox, as stubborn as a mule and as sly as a fox, but nevertheless, he answered to Fetcher's call.

Raising one eyelid he looked at Fetcher. Amos was sprawled back along a wooden chair with his salt-streaked black boots resting lazily on the table. At his side he had a pistol, loaded and ready for action.

'Yes, my man?' he drawled in a tired voice.

'Wake yerself up a bit. We needs to be alert!' Fetcher ordered, placing his cutlass by his side.

Amos grunted and put both his feet

back on the hewn stone floor.

'When the time comes, I'll be the first man on the beach, you see if I'm not.'

Both knew Amos would be the last, but they grinned at his boast. He would stay near to the inn. His job was to watch out and hide most of the contraband in his cellar.

Fetcher and Amos wrapped their black lengths of cloth around their necks. They would serve to protect their faces from the harsh, salt-laden winds and hide them in the dark.

'What if the revenue cutter's got 'em? That captain may tell on all of us. Then we'll hang for sure!'

Jack's voice was filled with fear as he spoke. He was the newest member of the group. His family had moved into the hamlet from a farm in the dales. He did not have natural sea legs or the ruthless character needed for such a desperate life.

'Cheer up, lad. You might be sent to the colonies instead, then you'd die slowly of fever in a strange land. So hanging's not that bad, is it? Anyway, dead's dead, lad. Don't matter where you are.'

Fetcher clenched his teeth as he glared at Amos.

'Keep watch, and stop yer frettin', lad. The captain knows 'is business. If the revenue cutter comes within 'is range he'll blast him and sink the cargo. He's the best. Like you said, the weather's bad this night. He may be late, but he'll come.'

Fetcher pulled on his brown woollen hat and continued to suck at his pipe. Amos was rubbing his hands against his striped waistcoat.

'Fanny, bring me some bread, lass.'

No sooner had he asked, than a pewter plate appeared on the hatch with a lump of stale bread on it and a jug of ale at its side. The arm that placed it there was pink, strong and ample like the rest of Fanny Barton. She was as hardworking as any of the fishermen's wives but Fanny, like Amos,

4

was shrewd. When the last owner of Monkton Manor, George Walton, had been arrested for stashing contraband, the revenue could not make any of the charges stick against the Bartons.

'The storm's gettin' worse, Fetcher. That mist's so thick now I can hardly see out,' Jack's voice droned on. 'It'll be nigh impossible gettin' the boats through the breakers and out to sea tonight. He'd better come soon.'

The youth fidgeted nervously as he sat watching. Fetcher glared at the boy's back. Jack could not see the hate in his eyes, but Amos could. Both men were as hard as nails, unlike the boy, whom Fetcher considered to be a liability. He was clumsy and prone to panic, a risk when in their business and there was no room for risks of any kind.

'No-one's got 'em, Jack. Be still and watch for the sign.'

Fetcher kept his voice calm, but he had already decided that Jack had to go. It was too profitable an operation to let one callow youth jeopardise it. He would wait his time.

He did not know if it would be tonight, but he knew his opportunity would come, and then Jack's time would run out.

Most honest men would be in bed, sound asleep, as the midnight hour passed. However, these were not honest men. In the eyes of His Majesty and his customs' office, they were villains, smugglers. They robbed the Crown of vital taxes needed for the prolonged war with France. Wages were meagre and taxes high, so these men risked their lives on the contraband run, to make more in one night than they could earn honestly in a week or longer.

'It's there! I see it, Fetch.'

Jack's voice was excited. He looked around for the lantern and was about to open both the wooden shutters wide when Fetcher slammed them firmly shut.

'Look to Stangcliffe. Wait for the sign!'

Jack returned to his post, unbowed

by Fetcher's rebuke but Amos shook his head malevolently at Fetcher. Both knew he could have them all hanged. They always waited for their lookout on the Stangcliffe headland, to signal the all-clear. They had to know if the preventative forces were waiting or else they would all be caught.

'Aye. I see it. Three swings and then two. It's clear, no revenue men here tonight.'

Jack's voice was filled with relief. Fetcher opened the shutters wide and the lantern was placed where Jack had been sitting. There were movements outside, as if the beach had suddenly come alive. Figures worked silently, efficiently, to manoeuvre three cobles, using two-wheeled trolleys to haul them to the water's edge.

Despite the storm they cut like a knife through the breakers. Cobles were the traditional, Yorkshire fishing boats. With their bows driven into the raging surf, they were perfect vessels for launching and landing a catch on open, flat beaches such as this one. Their large, rectangular lug sails were quick and easy to hoist because they had the minimum of rigging to deal with.

'Take care, lads,' Fanny's voice echoed from the back of the inn.

Fetcher smirked as Jack hesitated to give her a grateful smile. He knew she was not a sentimental woman but was highly superstitious. She always told them to take care. Fanny believed that if she did, they would come back with the contraband intact and she wanted her cut.

'The sea is a cold and merciless mistress, lad,' Fetcher added to Jack, not taking his eyes from Fanny.

The meaning, he had reason to know, applied equally to her. His comment was not lost on her, as she grinned broadly, revealing a mouth lacking in good teeth.

Jack pulled on his wool hat and ran down the beach, bracing himself against the cold sea mist and the freezing spray of the breakers. In his eagerness to get the job over with, he forgot his black scarf. His was the only face to show. Fetcher followed. His wiry frame and bandy legs gave a deceptive impression. He was a strong, accomplished sailor. He helped the three boats off the beach then ran back to the shelter of the inn. He watched the vessels tossed on the waves as they rowed out to the waiting lugger.

'Fanny, go now and tell the packers and the tubmen to come down.' Fetcher ordered.

Her large figure towered over him as she filled the doorway of the inn, wrapping herself in her woollen shawl. She pushed past him, deliberately rubbing her ample bosoms against him as she went by. Despite her bulk, she moved swiftly.

'Jack's an only son, Fetcher,' Amos said.

'That may be, Amos, but he's slow to learn and he panics. He'll have us all hanged if we keep him.'

Fetcher and Amos moved a cart out

from behind the inn and wheeled it on to the shore.

'Tonight then?' Amos asked as he pushed the cart down the beach.

'Aye, somehow.'

'Reckon they'll manage to unload the lugger OK?' Amos asked quietly, his voice covered by the sound of the crashing waves against the shore. 'It's rough an' the storm's gettin' worse.'

'Aye, they'll do well enough.'

The two men hunched close to each other, crouching behind the cart. They were as sheltered as they could be from the wind and driving rain, but there was no way of escaping the icy cold as it bit into these hardy men. Amos had his pistol tucked into his belt and both men were armed with knives and cutlasses.

By the time the tubmen returned with Fanny, from the cover of the wooded valleys, the cobles were approaching the shore. Silently and stealthily the men waited for their turn to unload the small barrels of brandy from France, Dutch gin, and fine silks for the city ladies. The tubmen were the farmers' hands who saw to the safe distribution of the goods, as they knew the paths through the woodland, across the open moors and down into the dales.

Seaham was a hive of activity under the daunting shadow of Stangcliffe. The boats were tossed about as they fought their way back to shore cutting like knives through the treacherous, inshore waters. Farther out, mountainous waves were building as the gale strengthened. They had to be quick. Everyone knew the chance of being caught tonight was slim but the risk to life from the elements was high.

'To the boats, men,' Fetcher snapped, forcing the tubmen to wade into the shallows to help the boats on to the waiting trolleys, ten to haul them ashore.

They were eager to make a quick profit. Soon they would disperse the contraband so it would vanish into the night without trace, as though it had never existed.

'A light, a light!' Jack's voice shrieked out as he jumped ashore.

Fetcher drew his pistol, clipping Jack hard around the back of his head as he did so with his other hand.

'Be still, you fool. Do you want the revenue down on us?'

Fetcher's voice was just loud enough for him to hear over the noise of the crashing waves.

'It's the vicarage. He'll see nowt and say nowt, unlike you!'

The miserable youth took the next barrel, placing it into the bottom of the waiting cart to haul to the inn. Fetcher released his grip on his pistol, not before having Jack temptingly within his sights.

'Curse him,' he growled, then saw to the smooth distribution of the goods. 'Jack, help Amos stash his brandy and gin in the tunnel then come and help me return this cart to the manor.'

The inn's cellar hid a secret tunnel, used as a store. Only Fetcher and Amos knew where the tunnel led and no-one dared ask them about it. When Jack returned to the beach, Fetcher was leaning hard into the wind, holding on to the cart.

'Move it, lad,' he ordered.

Jack didn't answer but grabbed the cart ready to start pushing it up the steep bank to Seaham itself.

'Here, lad. Don't forget this.'

Amos's huge figure had followed Jack. He pushed Jack's payment into his pocket. The lad smiled at him and sighed with relief as he felt the coins.

'Thanks, Mr B . . . '

'No names, no names!' Fetcher snapped.

The boy started to push the cart and Amos returned to the warmth of the inn. Fetcher leaned hard into the cart but let Jack take most of its weight. He'd put him on the outside as they pushed it around the steep bend that would take them up to the coach road which skirted the hamlet by the old Norman church. As they struggled to manoeuvre it around the bend of the track, the wind beat them mercilessly. The thick mist had been replaced by driving rain, making the going hard.

'Push, lad, push!' Fetcher ordered and, as Jack took the strain, he picked his pockets of his hard-earned coins and then stood aside.

The cart stopped momentarily as if stuck, then the force of its weight pushed downwards on Jack. The youth did not stand a chance. He was tired, wet and not strong enough to stand his ground. As it rolled back, he was forced farther and farther backwards towards the edge of the track, then the cart took him over the edge to the steep, rocky bank that led to the crashing waves below.

'Aagh . . . Fetcher!'

His scream was lost in the storm.

Fetcher grinned and braced himself as he inched towards the edge where Jack had been forced over. He'd heard the cart fall and pictured its splintering wood crashing, with Jack's broken body, against the jagged rocks below.

As Fetcher peered over the edge, he gasped, 'Saints be, lad, can yer not do anythin' right?'

The cart had knocked Jack hard and left him sprawled against a rock, but it had taken the full force of the fall itself. Jack was dazed, damaged, but still alive. He looked up with an expression of hope in his eyes as he focussed on Fetcher. Fetcher forced himself to stand as straight as he could in the wind. He looked around.

First he found a stone as big as his fist, then pulled out his cutlass. He used the latter to stake the land just above Jack's body, thus giving him something to steady himself with as he swung down with the rock, hitting the defenceless lad hard on the head before kicking his body off the boulder to join the cart in the murderous sea below. That done, Fetcher scrabbled back to his feet and returned to the inn.

'Here, Amos.'

Fetcher handed him half of Jack's coins.

'Ah, I love a job well done, Fetch.'

Amos grinned.

'You stayin' this night?'

'No, the boss'll want a report and I'll tell how we lost a man. Foul storm an' all, eh?' Fetcher said in mock humility.

'Aye, treacherous it was, not fit to be out in.'

Both men laughed as Amos opened the hatch to the cellar. Fetcher slipped behind a large barrel and disappeared into the tunnel. He had walked these passages as a child who had followed his father. Needing no light, he found his way up the steep steps to the safety of the stables at Monkton Manor.

This was the perfect place for him to be, as he slept in the small room at one end of the stable block. It was his private quarters as overseer of the estate and no-one, except the Master of Monkton Manor, dare enter unannounced.

'Man is meant to suffer for his sin and toil.'

Reverend Beckwith spoke with utter conviction.

'Life is not about making God's work easy.'

'Not all men have to toil though, do they, Reverend?' Megan Clegg asked and glanced at the large figure of Mr Eli Scafton who was sitting next to her on the coach's inadequate seat.

He had placed his ample rear there when he and his mouse of a wife had joined the coach at York. Mrs Amelia Scafton sat silently opposite him, next to Reverend Beckwith.

'There are more ways of toiling than through pure hard labour, my dear.'

He inclined his head towards Megan, peering over his small spectacles as he spoke to her.

'Some of us are called upon to serve Our Lord directly.'

'Aye, lass,' the voice of Eli boomed.

17

'And some of us are born to be leaders of men and rabble, like my good self and my woollen empire.'

Megan wondered how affluent his woollen empire was, but did not ask as Mrs Scafton managed to look at Megan for the first time, down her long, narrow nose. She, Megan thought, was proud of her husband's achievements in life.

Megan had stifled many a yawn as she listened to her companion on the long journey from Bristol to London, and then via York, onwards to the north-east hamlet of Seaham.

For most of the journey she had stared out of the coach window, taking in all the views of the land they passed through. Her excitement at this adventure was the only thing that made his interminable words of wisdom bearable. Reverend Thomas Beckwith continued his discussion with the gentlemen who had joined the coach at York.

'Now, I tell you, these mad men of

invention, they don't know a thing about the religion of decent folk, in my viewpoint.'

Eli Scafton was obviously glad of the receptive Reverend's attention. Megan was glad the two had each other to impress with their views, but wished they could do it somewhere else.

'What would my life be like if my weavers all wanted new-founded gadgets? It's preposterous! People are just plain lazy. They should do an honest day's work for a fair day's pay.'

He slapped his knee as he stressed his point, then belched at the effort.

'Look, Reverend, the coast.'

Megan pulled down the coach's small window only to be rebuked for letting in a chill wind, which could bring on one of Mrs Scafton's turns.

'We're nearing the sea!' Megan exclaimed as she pulled the window up again.

She was delighted to see they were following a rough road, which took them nearer the rugged and desolate coastline.

'How far are we from Seaham, Reverend Beckwith?' Megan asked, deliberately cutting across their conversation.

'Weather permitting, we should be there within the hour, my child,' Reverend Beckwith answered, as if appeasing her impatience.

Megan avoided eye contact with Mrs Scafton, who nodded in agreement to everything her husband said. Megan sensed the woman's disapproval of her, especially as she smiled every time the reverend called her 'child', as if sensing Megan's irritation.

'Take these fools who want to ban slavery,' Eli continued, not to be swayed.

This was too much for Megan. She was solidly behind those opposed to slavery. Having lived in Bristol she had seen too much of how the poor souls were treated, like the dregs of humanity.

'They're not dogs, but people. How

can we allow flesh and blood to be traded so cruelly, with mothers separated from their own children? It's inhumane.'

Megan blurted out her words with the passion she felt for the plight of those people. Her three companions turned and looked at her, aghast, not so much for what she had said, but for the way in which a nineteen-year-old, young lady should speak out so boldly, interrupting a man's discussion.

'My dear child,' Reverend Beckwith began in his usual patronising air, 'you speak of things that are beyond your understanding. Just as it would be wrong to attribute human feelings to a dog, we should not humanise these creatures. They need to toil to save themselves from the sinful lives they have led as heathens. God will judge them in His own time.'

Megan's cheeks glowed red as she tried to control her temper, and her tongue.

'Yes! Yes! Precisely, Reverend. They

need us to save them.'

Eli tried to look down at Megan but his stomach anchored him where he sat, his legs spread apart to leave room for his girth. Megan did not like his leg pressing against hers. His worsted tweed coat and hose were well made, but like the fat oaf that wore them, to Megan they stank. Reverend Beckwith sitting opposite him in his black sombre coat and old-fashioned tricorn hat was a thin twig of a man. This added to the serious, ill-looking demeanour of her companion.

Megan tried hard to control her temper.

'Surely people should be treated the same regardless of their creed or colour. Are we not taught to love our neighbour as ourselves?' Megan asked coyly.

'Goodness, girl, you've a lot to learn. Slaves are not our neighbours, and never shall be. You save your energy for finding yourself a good man and giving him plenty of sons. Leave politics to the men folk, lass.'

'Child, it is not your place to say such things,' Reverend Beckwith reprimanded her. 'Remember that a fool finds no pleasure in understanding, but delights in airing his own opinions. Mind my words.'

His attitude was too much for Megan's pride.

'I will, just as Proverbs tells us that reckless words pierce like a sword, whereas the words of the wise bring healing, I believe.'

Megan looked out of the coach window at the rough sea which had now come into full view.

She ignored the remonstrations and rebukes of her travelling companions and, instead of feeling cowed, pondered on how she could ever help the plight of slaves when a woman's place was so subordinate to that of such pompous men.

Women such as Mrs Scafton may pride themselves for their humility and obedience but Megan had other ideas.

She would bow to no man, other than out of respect. How she wished she had been born a boy. Then she could have taken over her father's inn when he died and his other business dealings. Instead, she was being chaperoned by an insufferably pious friend of her reverend uncle. How she missed her fun-loving, reckless father.

The coach crossed a headland revealing a flat, sandy bay. Tucked peacefully in the most sheltered part was an old inn behind which nestled a handful of fishermen's cottages. The headland of Stangcliffe overlooked the inn, which sat in the shadow of a small hill behind it. A small fleet of Yorkshire cobles was lined up along the shore.

Megan thought of the storm that had kept her awake the night before and looked out at the bay, now calm. The rain-filled darkness had now turned into a crisp, clear winter's day, the storm having blown itself out before dawn. Megan could see that the hamlet of Seaham was built on higher land, overlooking the bay.

'It's delightful!' she said, as she saw the old Norman church in front of the coach as it drew up.

The coach was welcomed by a handful of curious children and her reverend uncle and Aunt Elsie. She beamed at them as they opened the door, but before she had a chance to stand, Reverend Beckwith stepped down carefully to a rapturous welcome by her two only living relatives. Then, as if forgetting himself, Reverend Beckwith turned and said a fond farewell to the Scaftons.

'When I reach Newcastle I shall be sure to call in on you.'

'Please do, Reverend.'

Mrs Scafton smiled broadly at the prospect. To Megan, it appeared to be almost as an afterthought Reverend Beckwith offered his hand to Megan to help her down.

The coach driver, who had a scar on his cheek and a broken nose, unceremoniously threw Megan's bag to the ground. She was glad she did not have to see him again. Each time he smiled at her he had revealed a mouth of foul teeth and his eyes leered at her, making her cringe.

Megan stood there and watched the coach leave to rejoin the road that would take them on to Newcastle. Her aunt and uncle were in deep, animated conversation with the Reverend Beckwith who was divulging himself of all the trials and tribulations that had befallen him on their long journey. Megan had enjoyed every one of them except for his eternal preaching.

'Margaret, dear child, forgive me for being so overwhelmed to see my dear colleague and friend after all these years.'

Her uncle's rotund figure turned to her.

Megan instinctively held both her arms up to greet him, but he stopped in front of her and merely nodded.

'Did your father leave me a letter or

ask you to give anything to me, Margaret?'

Megan straightened and calmly lowered her arms. Her aunt stood behind her husband, making no move to embrace the niece she had never seen before.

'No, Uncle, but I don't think he expected to die so soon.'

Megan felt hurt by their cool reception and her quick wit got the better of her.

'We should all expect to die, Margaret. It is the one certainty each of us has to accept.'

Her uncle's sombre greeting was in stark contrast to the warmth of the welcome she had seen displayed towards Reverend Beckwith. Megan suspected her appearance in Seaham was not welcome.

'My father always called me Megan. That is my name, Uncle,' Megan said as calmly and sweetly as she could.

'He may have done so, as he did so many things. I, however, will not.

Margaret is what you were christened before Our Lord, and Margaret is what you will be called.'

Megan did not argue, not here in the open with people watching. Her aunt followed behind the two men as they turned and walked towards the house behind the church. It was only when the hooves of a horse were heard approaching them that they turned and realised she was still standing next to her bag.

Her uncle suddenly became animated and rushed over to her.

'My dear child, what will you think of us?'

He made a gesture to pick up her case.

'Fetcher! Carry the lady's case to the reverend's house.'

The order came from the rider of the beautiful black stallion. His master had equally dark hair and Megan could not help but notice when she looked up, ebony eyes. A large grey wolfhound trailed after him. Megan loved dogs and was taken by the animal's regal beauty. Megan became aware that his master was watching her.

A wiry, surly-looking man came forward from the wall of a cottage against which he had been leaning lazily. Megan did not like his shifty eyes and thought he looked weak, but he lifted the bag with no hardship and did his master's bidding.

'Master Samuel, thank you. This is my niece, Margaret, just arrived from Bristol.'

The reverend smiled up at the gentleman on horseback as he swung his leg casually in front of him and slipped off the horse with little effort.

'I'm pleased to make your acquaintance, miss. I will collect you after you have had time for a quick repast with your uncle.'

'Collect me?'

Megan was interrupted abruptly by her uncle.

'That will be very generous of you. I will see she is ready to meet your good lady mother. Do you require me to accompany her? I would gladly.'

'No, that will not be necessary. I can see her safely to the manor.'

Megan wondered why the handsome stranger should want to escort her to the manor. She watched dumbfounded as he remounted his horse in readiness to leave them. Her face flushed.

'Why would you wish to collect me to meet your mother?' she asked abruptly, looking from the rider to her uncle.

'Reverend, does the young lady understand our agreement?'

His voice sounded annoyed but as Megan stared up at his weather-tanned face, she thought she saw a flicker of a smile across it.

'My letter obviously did not arrive in time, but I assure you my niece will be ready after a light lunch.'

'Good.'

Without further hesitation, the rider, who was addressed as Master Samuel, rode off. Megan was not impressed by his well-worn coat, but his brown and tan boots, tack and horse were of the highest quality. Whoever he was, he represented the gentry and wealth. Her uncle had responded instantly to them, just as her father had often said he would. Her family had never been good enough for him.

'Come with me, Margaret.'

Her uncle cupped her elbow with his hand and walked her to their home. There she was requested to sit on a wooden chair by the fire, as he sat in a larger one at the other side. Reverend Beckwith was shown to his room for the night by her aunt.

'Now then, Margaret, I understood you to have been a well-groomed girl, although obviously some of your father's outspoken coarseness has come through in your blood.'

'I came here understanding I was to be welcomed into the home of my family,' Megan started but her uncle stood up and reached for his clay pipe off the ledge above the fire.

'You cannot stay here. There is no

room,' he blustered.

'Reverend Beckwith will be staying only the night.'

Megan could not understand what was happening.

'That room is needed. How can we offer hospitality if we have no bed free?'

He sat down again and started puffing on his pipe.

'By offering it to me,' Megan answered, her temper getting the better of her.

'You have been found a position above but hopefully not beyond your position in life. My, girl, the way you speak out you should be grateful for a position of scullery maid at the manor but I have managed to acquire for you the position of companion to Lady Mary Jarvis. She is the mistress of Monkton Manor and that gentleman you met is the master. He will be yours, too, and I trust you will be more civil in his presence than you were out there.'

Megan was speechless. She knew her uncle had disapproved of her father, but it never crossed her mind that she would not be welcome under his roof.

'What happens if the lady does not wish me for a companion, Uncle?' Megan asked.

'Then you had better find some more suitable, gainful employment more in keeping with your breeding. In short, Margaret, in your own interest, you had better not lose this chance to improve yourself. The suitable alternatives are by no means so numerous.'

Before Megan could reply, her uncle beamed at her and then at her aunt who was returning with Reverend Beckwith.

'Now, Elsie, take young Margaret to the kitchen and find her some food whilst I talk to my dear friend about his long and arduous journey. Master Samuel will return within the hour.'

His smile faltered slightly as he looked his wife straight in her eyes.

'Make sure your niece is ready for

him when he returns.'

Megan followed her aunt to the kitchen, where she was offered dry bread, cold meat and a small drink of milk.

'Aunt, can you not talk with him?' Megan asked, thinking she would try a humble approach as her aunt looked a kindly soul.

'Talk to whom, Margaret?'

'Uncle, to make him realise my home should be here, with you.'

Megan saw the kindly look that had shone so radiantly to Reverend Beckwith fade, to be replaced with unfeeling eyes.

'Girl, you do not know how hard your uncle has worked to attain this position for you at the manor. Do not be so ungrateful as to reject it. With a father like yours, you are lucky not to be down at the inn with the uncouth Bartons.'

'My name is Megan and my father, your brother, was a good man. He loved you.'

Megan thought she saw a glimmer of softness cross her aunt's face as she spoke of her father's affection for his younger sister.

'Perhaps he was once a good man and perhaps he did love me once, but that was before I was saved. Now I know better. Your father lived by the profit of selling illicit goods, yet he died a pauper. How so? Unless he gambled it, or worse, spent it on lewd women.'

Her aunt paused as if waiting for Megan to explain how her father's wealth had vanished. Megan said nothing but remembered her uncle's first question to her on meeting. They may not have approved of his lifestyle but they wanted the residue. Megan thought they would have to want. To the world, she was the orphan of a man who lived beyond his means and died penniless.

Only she knew differently, but for now she had to fulfil her rôle and if that meant spending hours listening to the ranting of some old woman in a rotting old manor then so be it. She would never confide in her aunt and uncle. In silence she ate her food and waited for her new master to return.

2

Megan sat in silence as she ate. Her aunt busied herself serving the good reverends with a hot stew and her freshly-baked bread. She ignored Megan completely until she, too, sat down at the kitchen table to eat a piece of her bread on which she had ladled some gravy from the stew.

'So, Margaret, you must be ready to be on your best behaviour for Master Samuel.'

Her aunt stared intensely at her, obviously ill at ease.

'What learning do you have, girl?'

'Learning, ma'am?'

Megan adopted the air of a humble servant. Whatever learning she had, she would not share with these people. She decided that the least they knew about her the better. After all, their minds were firmly closed to her and her past.

Her father may not have been a God-fearing man, but he knew how to love and respect people, his daughter above all.

'Yes, learning. Did my brother have you instructed as to the ways of a lady? It's not proper for you to understand too much of the ways of the world. However, you should have been instructed as to the place of a lady.'

Her aunt's head lifted and froze with her spoon halfway between the pewter plate and her mouth. A sudden look of concern crossed her face, and then she appeared to regain her composure.

'Yes, of course you have. The way you carry yourself is correct. Mind your manners at the manor. Your uncle has staked his reputation on it. He has a position to uphold in this community. Do nothing to discredit it, girl.'

Her aunt stared at her with grey eyes that had a steely, threatening determination about them, and left the room for a moment to return, clutching a black shawl.

'You should wear this when Master Samuel returns for you. It is far more fitting than your pelisse, which is of a quality that is far beyond your social status.'

Her aunt stroked Megan's pelisse, as it lay over the back of a kitchen chair as if claiming it as her own.

'A girl should not flaunt her figure or her God-given looks when she is to go into the service of a respectable household.'

Megan was angered if her aunt thought for one moment she would leave one of her father's precious gifts for her. She would be very mistaken. Megan did feel a sense of pity towards her aunt though, as she perceived the older woman's jealousy of her youth. But before Megan could respond, there was a loud knock on the vicarage door. Her aunt jumped up to answer it promptly. Megan carefully folded her pelisse and put it into her bag with her other personal and precious belongings.

Then she followed her aunt into the living-room where her uncle remained huddled in his wooden chair by the fire. Reverend Beckwith was standing with his back to her, warming his hands by the open fire. Both men turned and looked at Megan as her aunt re-entered the room.

'Master Samuel has arrived for Margaret.'

Megan looked at the pride showing itself in her aunt's face as Elsie held her hands nervously in front of her. They obviously wanted to have a niece situated in the manor. Megan was tempted to deliberately throw the opportunity back at them by behaving inappropriately, but realised her uncle was serious about finding her a less suitable position.

'Good, good, well invite him in.'

Her uncle stood up immediately and Megan reflected how he was so short and round he almost looked like a cartoon drawing of the vicar he was.

'He has sent his man, Fetcher, to the

door to collect Margaret,' Aunt Elsie added.

Megan saw a look of disappointment cross her uncle's face, but it was replaced quickly by an animated gesture of scurrying Megan to the door.

'Dear child, you must not keep your new master waiting. Come.'

He walked her with his hand placed firmly on the crook of her elbow towards the waiting coach. Fetcher overtook them, carrying Megan's bag and loaded it on to the seat next to his and picked up the reins.

As they approached the carriage, her uncle leaned close to her and said, 'Margaret, I hope you truly appreciate the opportunity I have given you here to improve yourself and put your past behind you. Do not dishonour yourself or us.'

Her uncle's face stared determinedly ahead and smiled broadly as the coach door opened. Samuel Jarvis stepped out, unfolding a step for Megan to use to climb into it. Megan admired his tall figure. He had an air of confidence about him that comes from being in control of your life. Few, Megan thought, had that privilege, including herself.

'Master Samuel, Margaret now understands and is quite eager to meet your good lady mother and take up her new position. Aren't you, dear?'

He looked at her pointedly.

'It is true that I cannot wait to leave here and see the manor, Uncle,' Megan said pleasantly and with a forced smile.

She may not like the manor but it was the most honest thing she could say under the circumstances for she had no wish to stay where she was not wanted.

Samuel looked down at her as if sensing her meaning. He held her gaze for a moment as if searching her soul. She looked straight back into his eyes, deep, ebony pools, before deciding she should avert her eyes rather than challenge the man under whose roof she had been forced to live.

'Thank you, Reverend. I will come by tomorrow to discuss our business,' Samuel said whilst he held the door open for Megan to climb in.

'Reverend Tully! Reverend Tully!'

All three turned as one of the village women ran up, obviously flustered.

'Sorry to interrupt.'

She glanced nervously at Samuel Jarvis and dipped a slight curtsey as she said, 'Sorry, your lordship, for disturbing you but it's my Jack.'

Reverend Tully looked at her with what Megan could only assume to be genuine concern.

'What's the matter with Jack, Betty?' he asked.

''E's missin' an' I can't find 'im anywhere. Nobody 'as seen 'im since 'e left the inn last night.'

Samuel looked at the woman.

'I'll ask at the manor for you and send him back if he's sleeping off a hangover somewhere.'

''E's a good lad, our Jack. E'd not run off or do owt wrong.'

She looked pleadingly at Reverend Tully.

'Goodbye, Margaret. You'd best be going now and I'll help Betty find young Jack.'

Megan climbed into the carriage. She heard Samuel shout to Fetcher to ask if he'd seen the lad, but he must have just shrugged his shoulders, as she heard no reply. Samuel climbed in, sitting opposite her in the small carriage.

As it pulled away and started on the journey to Monkton Manor, leaving behind the old church and hamlet of Seaham, she averted her eyes to stare out of the small window. Megan could sense Samuel's eyes on her. She resented him as much as she resented being made to take a position in his household. She had always been free, and freedom, Megan knew, was a thing to be treasured. One day, she would return to London, then Bristol, and have enough money to live a free life of her own, but now she would be a servant.

'How old are you, Margaret?'

His voice was strong, not gentle and prying. It lacked subtlety. It was firm and was used to being answered and obeyed, of that she had no doubt.

'I am nineteen, and if it please you, your lordship, would you call me Megan? It is what I am used to.'

Megan avoided eye contact with him. His presence unnerved her but she must not show it. She could not be his equal, but hated the idea of being his or anybody's servant.

Megan had to control her temper and pride. It was a struggle not to look directly at him. She must learn to at least act subservient or she could end up on the streets. Megan needed time above all else, and then she would no longer need her position or family.

'Megan!' he shouted loudly and in a sharp voice, which made her jump and stare straight at him.

A grin crossed his face and for a moment she sensed her eyes flashed annoyance at him.

'Now I have your attention, you would perhaps do me the honour of answering some questions.'

He leaned back into the seat, resting an elbow on the small window in the carriage door, his legs crossed comfortably. Megan sat primly with her hands folded in each other on her lap. She sat upright and tried to soften the look in her eyes and her voice.

'Indeed, if it pleases, I shall answer your questions.'

Megan now looked into his dark eyes. Pools, she thought, deep, dark, dangerous pools.

'Good, I'm glad you are so concerned about what pleases me. Stay that way and it shall be well with me. Have you been a lady's companion before?'

'No, your lordship,' she answered honestly.

As he sighed and looked out of the window, she noticed the neat black leather tie, which held his hair together at the nape of his neck. She pictured him in a naval officer's uniform and thought he would cut a fine figure. Had he fought in the wars with France? There were many questions she would like to ask him. No doubt in time she would find out.

'Are you able to sew or embroider, read, write or ride?' he inquired.

'Yes, milord,' she answered briefly and noted his eyebrows rise immediately.

'Which one or ones?'

'All, milord.'

Megan did not change her expression or manner. She was careful not to sound overconfident or boastful.

'Tolerably well?' he added still looking quite surprised at his new member of staff.

'Yes, tolerably.'

'What was your father, Megan, and how long since did your mother pass away?' he continued.

Although her initial surprise that the master of the manor should have bothered himself to collect her, Megan could now see that he had fully intended to interview her himself before she had any chance of seeing his mother. Megan wrapped her aunt's shawl more tightly around her, without realising what she was doing as she shifted uneasily on the seat.

'Are you cold, Megan?'

He pulled up the small window on the coach by its leather strap.

'No,' Megan said brightly, 'just a shiver,' and realised that she was nervous about answering personal questions relating to her family.

She had to stay calm.

'My father owned a coffee house and inn in Bristol and my mother died when I was but a child of five.'

'What was the name of the coffee house?' he asked with a keen look.

'Do you know Bristol, milord?' she responded innocently, trying to distract him from asking such pointed questions.

'Yes. Which house was it?'

'The Southern Star.'

48

'By the waterfront?'

He grinned momentarily.

'So where was the inn?'

'The Flagon, in the city. It was well frequented by the merchants who trade there,' Megan said, showing pride in her father's achievements.

'So you are more than an innkeeper's daughter.'

Megan's chin rose, as did her gaze, which had wandered to the change of scenery as the coach road took them away from the coast and into the comparative shelter of a valley. It fixed firmly on to Samuel Jarvis's arrogant face. She had no doubt as to what his question implied as to her suitability for a companion to a born lady.

'My father owned a respectable inn, and a coffee house; in which a fair deal of trade would be carried out. I have never worked in either, milord, however, I respected my father deeply for the good man he was. I had a governess who taught me the ways of a lady and my father who taught me to read and write.'

'I'm pleased to hear it.'

There was a dry sarcasm to his voice which caused Megan's cheeks to flush. She tried to distract herself by poking a rebellious curl back into her bonnet. Then her annoyance changed to embarrassment as she realised he was watching her.

'If Mother decides you will do, I will expect you to attend to her needs, accompany her on outings and read to her at her will. You will attend church with her each Sunday morning and, if it pleases her, you may visit your uncle and aunt for a short while then. Now read this to me.'

From his pocket he produced a piece of paper. Megan looked at it and read out the words which were taken from a passage in the Bible.

'You read well, but where was it from?' he asked when she had finished.

'The Bible,' she answered simply, and was amused by his sigh.

'Can you be more specific?'

'First Corinthians, Chapter Thirteen, but I am unsure of the verse number.'

'Very well.'

He glanced out of the window and leaned forward with his elbows resting on his legs and his hands loosely together.

'I will introduce you to my mother and it is up to you to impress her. Do you have any suitors anywhere?'

He had saved this last and unexpected question until they had turned on to a long, tree-lined drive that led to a small, hump-back bridge over a small river.

'No, none.'

He raised his eyebrows in a small gesture of surprise.

'Good. Whilst you're here your focus should be firmly on the well-being of my mother, for which you will receive the agreed remuneration. You shall have one day off per month, which will be at the discretion of my mother.'

'Remuneration?' Megan repeated.

'Yes, agreed with your uncle. Did he

not tell you? He offered to keep it safe for you, to be paid to him.'

The coach stopped and he placed his hand on the handle ready to open the carriage door.

'To be paid to me, please, milord,' Megan said in the most confident manner she could muster without hoping to sound arrogant.

He paused momentarily, as if thinking.

'I shall inform your uncle that we have agreed I keep your remuneration safely in my office until such time as you need it. Does that meet with your satisfaction, Margaret?'

He looked directly into her face. She could smell his cologne and his presence was affecting her in a strange way.

'Yes, thank you, and please, call me Megan.'

As she spoke, he climbed out and held her hand as she stepped down to her first sight of Monkton Manor. Her attention was completely distracted, not only by the manor, but by a large grey wolfhound bounding over to Samuel's side. By the look on both their faces, master and hound had a deep affection for each other.

Megan was so in awe of the manor house's stark beauty that she was almost unaware that Samuel had been speaking to her.

'Sorry, milord?'

She looked up at him as he stood head and shoulders above her.

'I said, Megan, I will give you your family name, if you will call me Mr Samuel and not milord. I own a manor house but have no title. However, my mother is a lady and you will refer to her as Lady Mary.'

'Yes, mi . . . Mr Samuel.'

He strode off through the large doors. Fetcher took her bag in and she followed slowly. Monkton Manor was not the largest of manor houses but it stood in a valley behind the hill that shadowed Seaham and the high ridge of Beckton Moor. To the left was a large stable block and to the right a large barn.

Sheep grazed on the fields surrounding the manor, so Megan had no doubt that this was a working farm. The house was grey and imposing, with chimneys that reached high into the sky. Yet Megan sensed its tranquillity. It was sheltered from both the harsh North Sea winds and gales and the open moor. Monkton Manor's buttresses stood proud, and so did Megan as she held her head high and entered the hall.

3

Megan entered the building and was instantly taken by how light the inside was. She was faced by the striking figure of Samuel Jarvis who was standing waiting for her to enter, his hound at his side.

Megan blushed slightly as he watched her look around her, staring firstly at the stone floor entrance as she moved forward on to the marbled flooring of the grand hallway. Two columns, also of marble, stood either side of an old, oak staircase. The walls were coloured in a rich, refreshing cream adding to the feeling of space and light.

'Megan, you can wait in the old hall. My mother will send for you presently.'

He gestured towards the double oak doors, which were to her right. Samuel opened one without entering.

'Make yourself comfortable.'

She entered the grand hall where a long, oak table that looked centuries old took pride of place in the centre of the panelled room. Although surrounded by wood, the room was light because of the large, rectangular windows that looked out on to the drive by which the coach had just brought them. Opposite the windows was a large, stone, carved fireplace above which was hung a family coat of arms.

Megan turned to ask if they were Samuel's own when she realised he had left her on her own. She stared at the settee and wondered if she should sit down by the open fireplace, where embers still flickered in the hearth. She stopped and picked up one of the tapestry cushions. They were exquisitely made.

'Do you enjoy needlepoint, girl?'

The sharpness of the voice gave Megan a start.

'I admire the quality of workmanship of this standard, milady,' she answered automatically.

Megan replaced the cushion carefully and stared at the elegant lady who was now entering the room, dressed in a pale lemon, high-waisted silk dress, which was delicately embroidered with intricate flowers all over the draped material.

Far from being a doddering, old lady, this lady had hair as dark as Mister Samuel's and the features were unmistakenly similar. Megan was sure she could only be Lady Mary Jarvis. She did not want to tell her honestly how she hated wasting her time on embroidery when she could ride, walk, read or just enjoy being alive.

Megan instinctively wrapped her aunt's old shawl around her shoulders as it had slipped off, revealing her neck and the fine lace edging of her own pale green cotton dress. The styles of the two women's garments were similar, however, the quality put them classes apart.

'Did you not hear my question or did you deliberately choose not to answer it?'

Lady Mary walked gracefully farther into the room. She had the deportment and attitude of the aristocracy, Megan thought. She swallowed her pride and determined to humble herself. Megan knew she had to. At the very least, she must win this woman's forbearance, or approval. This, she pondered, would not be easy. Megan tried to look as innocent and naïve as she could. She told herself to think like a servant. This graceful, forceful, beautiful mature woman was her better. Megan repeated the words to herself. Somehow she had to believe them and not rebel.

'Yes, milady, I do enjoy some needlepoint.'

She tried not to stare at the intricate plait and curls of the dark hair that sat on Lady Mary's head. A feeling of inadequacy deepened within her as she prayed she would not be asked to fix her hair. She had enough trouble controlling her own wilful locks.

'What can you tell me about the

tapestry on the wall, girl?' the lady asked her.

Megan sensed an intensity about the woman as she stared at Megan as if trying to unnerve her. Megan turned to see the most beautiful tapestry she had seen for a long time. Being the daughter of someone she had been told was a merchant and an enterprising man who had made a small fortune from contraband, she was familiar with many luxuries and artefacts.

'Why it's beautiful and Belgian, milady.'

When Megan turned around Lady Mary was sitting on the sofa. A maid entered the room and put a silver tray, on which lay a book, on top of a table at the end of the settee. She then stoked the fire, curtsied and left. Megan stood uncomfortably, not sure what to do next, whilst the lady picked up the book and handed it to her.

'What is that?'

Mary's eyes were as sharp as any knife. Megan sensed the astuteness of this woman and decided not to say the obvious, a book!

'It is the book of Robinson Crusoe as written by Daniel Defoe. I understand it is based on a true story about a shipwrecked man, who befriended a native.'

Megan handed it back but noticed a raised eyebrow when she used the word native as opposed to savage.

'Do you read French or Latin?'

'No, ma'am. I can speak a degree of French but know no Latin, worth mentioning.'

'So why do you want to be a lady's companion?'

Again the question was stark and pointed.

'It is a good position for a girl to be fortunate enough to have, milady.'

Megan stumbled slightly over her words. She was lying because she hated the idea. A servant was a servant and she had been used to her freedom, but she needed time so she had to swallow her pride and be grateful to her uncle for this appointment.

'You lie abysmally, which is good. I'll know when you are being dishonest. Your uncle and my son have acted in a conspiracy in order to establish you here for my benefit. Well, girl, you are not needed, but since I was inconvenienced by a fall recently, my son has decided that I need a nursemaid. Like it or not you will be that maid and now you will take off that motley-looking shawl and burn it on the fire before it offends my eyes anymore.'

'But it belongs to my aunt. She insisted I wore it,' Megan said as she carefully folded it up.

'Good, at least, you're not a wasteful girl. However, I shall have it returned to your aunt with my condolences.'

The lady grinned to herself and then eyed Megan up and down, as she stood there by the fire in her pale green dress.

'Take off that miserable hat, also.'

'My father died six months since. I wore the sombre hat out of respect, ma'am.'

Megan removed her hat and held it loosely in her hands in front of her. Her dark auburn hair seemed to come alight with a flicker of the hearth flames.

'Throw it on the fire and say goodbye now to whatever ghost of unhappiness remains within you, for I shall not have a broody chick clucking at my side.'

Megan hesitated.

'Throw it now!'

Mary's sharp tone made the request an order not to be refused. Megan threw the hat, her symbol of mourning, into the fire and watched it burn, as if transfixed, until Samuel's voice broke into her thoughts of her dear father and the fun life she had always shared with him.

'So, Mother, are we to keep Megan now she has no shawl or hat to wear, or do we throw her out into the streets?'

Samuel's question was obviously full of sarcasm, and they both laughed as Megan looked aimlessly from one to another before her cheeks burned slightly with indignation and her eyes started to flash with a tinge of anger.

'We'll keep her, for now.'

The lady stood up and spoke as if Megan were not even in the room.

'Have her fed and shown to her room. In one hour we shall see how well she reads.'

Samuel nodded to his mother in acknowledgement of her wishes and watched as she left the room. He remained, staring at Megan in a manner which to Megan seemed both offensive and intrusive.

'Fetcher has taken your bag up to your room already. I'll show you where it is. A tray will be brought up to you.'

Without thinking, Megan did not follow him as he moved towards the doorway, she merely answered, 'I have already eaten at my uncle's house.'

He did not look back at her.

'You may have, but I doubt it would compare with a warm meal here, from Betsy, our cook. Come, Megan.'

Samuel kept walking and led Megan up the central staircase. She felt she had no choice but to follow him. Her life was now under the direction and whim of these total strangers.

To the right of the stairs, Samuel opened a bedroom door. Inside Megan could see a mahogany-framed, four-poster bed. Its dark colour was in stark contrast to the bright canary-yellow walls and cream drapes, which hung at the long window. Without waiting she walked in and stared out at the view down the valley. She took a sharp intake of breath. It was, however, completely opposite to the views she was used to.

How she missed the view from her old window in Bristol, and the smells of the spices being unloaded and the aroma of coffee beans, but then she sighed as she remembered the not-so-sweet smells of the slave ships unloading a pathetic, desperate cargo. This view was untainted and fresh. She was suddenly aware of Samuel standing behind her. She smelled his cologne and for some inexplicable reason wanted to rest her head on his chest as she stared out at a new world to her.

'Do you find your room suitable?' Samuel asked as he placed one hand on her shoulder.

'It is fine.'

She spoke quickly and turned away from him. Her bag had been put on an old oak chest at the end of her bed. She pulled nervously at the buckle of the leather strap that had held it secure on her journey, only it held fast. It had become saturated by rain and had locked in place as it dried.

Samuel took hold of it and pulled it free. He was strong, Megan could see, as the buckle and strap opened along with the bag. Megan closed it tight quickly. She saw a grin pass Samuel's face. Perhaps he thought she was embarrassed in case her undergarments fell out of her reticule. Megan thought he could think what he liked so long as he stayed out of her things.

'I'll leave you to unpack,' he said firmly. 'Megan,' he went on and waited for her to look up into his eyes, 'your food will be sent up presently, be so good as to eat it. Pride has many pitfalls, hunger would be such a foolish one to fall into.'

Without waiting for her to reply, he left. Within ten minutes a tray was brought with the sweetest-smelling soup she had ever savoured. She then ate the poached salmon and drank the warmed milk. Neatly folded in a napkin was a warm bread bun. She ate her fill and was truly grateful that Samuel had ignored her protestations, even though she hated being talked to as a child. Megan decided it was an annoying habit he had.

She was then summoned to Lady Mary's room. To her surprise the man, Fetcher, whom she disliked on sight, was the servant who took her there. Elegantly draped on a crimson chaise by the large windows was Lady Mary.

'Thank you, Fetcher, and please have my horse ready in two hours.'

Fetcher bowed and Megan thought he had a relaxed air about him, which he had not displayed when in the presence of Mister Samuel.

'Yes, milady,' he answered and smiled broadly before closing the doors.

'Now, Margaret, you may read to me. I'll stop you when I've had enough and you can help to change me for a ride. You do ride, don't you?'

'Yes, milady.'

Megan sat on the window seat as Lady Mary had gestured to her. She picked up the book and started to read. After two chapters she stopped, as it seemed to her the lady was asleep. The gold chain and amber pendant that hung around Mary's neck caught her attention. It was exquisite, like the owner, although now she was close to her she could see the signs of her age, the wrinkles on her hands, the lines on her face around her eyes and neck. She carried her years well but time could not be turned back, not even for the idle rich, Megan reflected.

'Did I tell you to stop, girl?'

Mary did not open her eyes but the

words were stark and pointed.

'No, milady.'

Megan started to read again.

'Then why did you?' her voice interrupted Megan.

'Sorry, ma'am.'

Megan started to read once more.

'What did I ask you, girl?'

Megan put the book down on her lap and watched the lady open her eyes and stare directly at her. Megan did not flinch.

'I was admiring your necklace, ma'am.'

'Why?'

'Because it is so beautiful and well made,' Megan replied honestly.

Mary laughed and stood up.

'Do you think I would wear anything of poor quality?'

'No, ma'am.'

Mary opened a drawer and pulled out a pale blue shawl edged simply with a silver thread.

'This is not of a suitable quality.'

She threw it over to Megan.

'You use it for our walks.'

'Thank you, milady.'

Megan tried to sound genuinely grateful, trying to ignore the temptation to throw it back.

'Now I tire of reading. Change me for riding.'

Megan soon learned that Lady Mary was given to impulse. She rode daily and enjoyed bursts of energy as much as her long periods of rest. Samuel kept himself busy on the estate, but dressed for dinner each evening and was polite and attentive on conversation.

Two days later, Lady Mary had asked to be changed for riding earlier than usual. Megan was sent to the stable block to shout to Fetcher to bring the horses around to the front of the manor. As she approached the stables, she thought she heard voices. Instinctively she walked stealthily towards the open stable door. One of them was Fetcher.

'E's been found. So? No matter.'

His voice was in hushed tones but

Megan recognised it. As she entered the stables, one of the horses whinnied. Fetcher instantly appeared at the end of the stable block. He looked annoyed.

'This is no place for you. Your place is in the manor.'

His voice was definite, brusque even.

'Lady Mary sent me to ask you to get the horses. We are ready for our ride now.'

'I'll be there in a moment.'

He stared at her and Megan realised she was obviously expected to leave. As she walked away there were no other voices heard. Fetcher appeared shortly afterwards with two magnificent animals. He watched her as she walked back to Lady Mary, who was staring intensely at her, as if trying to intimidate her.

'What took you so long, girl?' Mary snapped.

'She gave me a start, ma'am, coming into the stables like that,' Fetcher said and side glanced at Mary, as he spoke.

'I told you to shout for Fetcher, not

go snooping!' Mary snapped at Megan.

'Sorry, ma'am, I didn't think it right for me to shout and I thought I heard Mr Fetcher talking in the stables.'

Megan watched the smirk on Fetcher's face disappear. He was hiding something for sure, but what?

'If I tell you to shout, it is not your position to doubt my order, do you understand?'

Mary's vexed voice surprised Megan.

'Were you talking to someone?' Mary asked Fetcher.

'No, just me'self, ma'am,' Fetcher said then, as if as an afterthought, added, 'I did hear how Atkins' new foal died. Sad that.'

Mary grunted as if in comprehending agreement.

'Shall I ride today or stand here surrounded by incompetent servants?'

With that, the two ladies mounted their horses and started trotting down the drive. Fetcher followed at a distance behind them.

'Now what?'

Mary's mood had changed into one of poor temper. Megan rode silently alongside. Within a very short time of being at Monkton Manor she realised that, whilst the food and accommodation were very pleasing, her ladyship was a person not to be vexed.

Megan looked down the long drive, hoping they would ride towards the coast. She both loved and missed the sea. Her thoughts were interrupted when she saw a figure riding towards them.

Wearing a hat, dark coat and pale breeches, he cut a dashing figure as he rode up to them.

'Ladies.'

He smiled and lifted his hat. His white silk cravat framed a square jawbone. His fair hair was cut fashionably to the neck and was the opposite in colour and style to that of Samuel Jarvis.

'Sir,' Mary greeted him as she held her horse steady, 'who has the pleasure of addressing me?'

Her brusque manner was only softened by a faint smile. Fetcher had caught up with the group and hung behind, but within earshot.

'My name is Timothy Spencer-Hughes.'

He paused as Samuel rode down from the fields.

'Sir,' Hughes acknowledged Samuel, 'I was just introducing myself. I am Timothy Spencer-Hughes.'

'And what business brings you here, Mr Spencer-Hughes?' Lady Mary asked.

'I work for HM Customs service. I came to talk to a Mister Samuel Jarvis of the Manor,' the stranger explained.

'I am Mr Jarvis. However, I have an urgent matter to attend to at the moment. Can you make a more convenient appointment to visit?' Samuel replied brusquely.

Mary turned her horse around. She smiled broadly at the revenue man.

'Come, Mr Spencer-Hughes, or may I call you Timothy?'

'Of course, ma'am.'

'Come, Timothy. You shall take refreshments with us whilst Samuel attends to his urgent business. Then you two can become better acquainted.'

Megan looked at Samuel's face. His normally dark eyes were darkened further by suppressed anger as his mother spoke. He angrily kicked his horse off.

'Fetcher, I'll need your help.'

Fetcher followed but Megan wondered what was going on in that weasel of a man's mind as he, too, glowered at the back of the revenue man, as he rode towards the house with Mary. Megan walked her horse behind Lady Mary and thought she had found herself in the middle of a household that was far from the tranquil hollow she had initially thought that it was.

4

Megan tried to listen to as much conversation as she could as they walked the horses back down the drive to the manor. Mr Spencer-Hughes was quick to dismount and offer his help to Lady Mary.

'Timothy, could you stay and join us for dinner?'

Megan watched as Lady Mary asked her question with the most charming and welcoming of smiles.

'I would be honoured, Lady Mary, to join two of the most beautiful ladies I have encountered since arriving in these parts.'

For a moment, Megan did not realise he was referring to her as well until she caught a rather piercing stare from Mary.

'Of course, my new companion-maid, Megan, shall join us.'

Mary turned to her, and a genuine smile had crossed her face as she looked at Spencer-Hughes studying Megan. She wondered how Mary's mood, which had started out so foul, could turn sweet so easily. Megan thought this lady could be harder to judge than a storm at sea.

Mr Spencer-Hughes moved forward to help Megan down when Mary interrupted his intentions.

'Megan, ride to Mr Samuel and tell him he will need to be prompt for dinner. We have a guest. Firstly, take my horse to the stable and inform Fetcher to see to it. Megan, be prompt about it.'

'I could do that, milady,' Spencer-Hughes offered but Mary was quick to respond.

'No! No! You are our guest, Timothy. Whatever would people say?'

Mary held out her hand and the tall, slim figure of Mr Hughes took it, but paused in order to nod politely to Megan first, before leading Mary into the manor.

Megan held tight to the reins of Mary's fine mount and led it back to the stable block. Tethering her own mount firmly she walked Mary's horse back into its stable. Despite her best intentions not to, she looked to the end where Fetcher had appeared. Quickly, she peeped back outside. A maid crossed from the dairy to the kitchen door, then there was no-one.

She ran to the opposite end of the block to see half a dozen stairs rising to an open room. She dared herself to climb up them and peek over the top step. A narrow palette strewn with blankets was against the outer wall. To the right, a locked chest nestled next to a three-legged stool to its side. Pipes lay on a dish on the small table at the bedside. There was no other way out than the way in which she had entered, yet something felt suspicious to her.

The voices she had heard before were real, so where had the second voice come from? No-one else had entered or left whilst she was in the yard. She was climbing backwards down the open stairs, being careful not to trip on her hem, when something caught her eye. She could see an object tucked under the bed.

A feeling of panic filled her as, against her commonsense, she went up to investigate. Wrapped in an oilcloth was a pistol and pushed farther under, a black neck cloth. Odd place to keep it, she thought. Megan felt a cold fear run through her. She mustn't get caught here. Without hesitation she made her way back along the stable block and only resumed a calm pace when she re-emerged into the yard to remount her horse.

Then, as if making up for the time she had spent snooping, she kicked her horse to a trot over the bridge and before realising what she was doing, made straight for the ridge. Megan was invigorated by the ride and enjoying the exhilaration of galloping across the open field to where Mr Samuel and Fetcher were talking to a man by the roadside.

Megan reined in her mount and walked it up to the small group of men. She suddenly became self-conscious as wisps of her hair surrounded her face. She tried to contain it by tucking a few curls quickly behind her ear with one finger. It was a simple enough gesture for her curls to ignore.

'Mister Samuel, Lady Mary requests your company for dinner as you have a guest.'

Megan steadied her horse and caught her breath. She was sure there was no way that Fetcher could tell she had been in his room, but the man looked at her with such scathing that she sensed she would have to watch her back where he was concerned.

She continued, 'Milady also requests that Fetcher stables her horse.'

'Who is our guest, or is it too obvious an answer?'

Samuel looked down at his hand as he fingered the reins, in apparent agitation.

'Mr Timothy Spencer-Hughes,' Megan answered.

'Fetcher, see to the horse.'

He turned to the man standing resting on a walking-stick by the road.

'Jason, tell Reverend Tully I shall pay my respects to Jack's family tomorrow.'

As he said this, Fetcher walked his horse forward alongside Megan and before kicking it into a gallop, he said, 'Mr Fetcher, to you!'

She ignored him and was sure that Mr Samuel had not heard him. Megan felt she should also have ridden back but something inside her made her stay. She could see the concern in Samuel's face and turned her horse as he walked his forward, falling in line with each other.

'Has something happened, Mr Samuel?' Megan enquired, remembering the overheard conversation in the stable block.

'Yes, something's happened,' he repeated and kicked his horse on to a gallop making no effort to explain to her what.

Megan followed and did not stop until they reached the bridge. She wondered if Jack had been found, as their horses fell into step again.

'You ride well, Megan. Did your father teach you that also?' Samuel asked and looked at her.

A glimmer of a smile appeared on his face, as he seemed to focus on her hair and not her face.

'Yes, he did. He loved getting away from the city once a month and we would ride in the countryside around Bath, then take the waters.'

She felt a surge of happiness as she remembered those days of laughter and pure joy.

Samuel's eyes smiled back at her, as he stopped and dismounted outside the stables.

'We have a guest to see to. You had better attend your mistress, Miss Tully.'

Megan opened her mouth to correct him, and tell him she was not Megan

Tully but Megan Clegg. Fetcher joined them to take the horses into the stable. Samuel Jarvis walked back to the manor, his stride determined and angry. She had no wish to be left in Fetcher's company so she entered the manor via the kitchen.

Turning left swiftly, as quietly as she could and avoiding the cook who was in a fluster organising dinner, she tiptoed up the servants' staircase, which emerged at the other side of the landing to her room and next to Lady Mary's.

Megan decided that, with a revenue officer in the manor, it was better to be Megan Tully, niece of a respectable reverend than Megan Clegg, daughter of the late Mad Jack Clegg, a man of undetermined means, accused of smuggling, but never ever caught and tried. As she emerged from the staircase, Mary's voice echoed through her door.

'Good of you to return, girl!'

Her mood was acidic again, but Megan wondered, as she entered Mary's room, how on earth she had known Megan was there.

After an hour of preparation and dressing by Megan and a maid called Annie, Lady Mary was finally pleased with her appearance. She had chosen an elegant cream gown and fine silk shawl that was decorated with gold thread. Dark curls hung down her face, which showed no blemish through its make-up. She stood up and looked in horror at Megan who was still wearing a riding outfit, not at all the suitable attire for dinner with a guest.

'Goodness, girl, you will not sit at my table dressed like that!'

Mary gestured towards the door.

'Go and get your best silk dinner dresses and I shall pick one that is suitable.'

Megan paused. In order not to seem too affluent, she had packed but a few cotton day dresses, keeping her finery to a minimum.

'Silk, ma'am?'

Megan deliberately fidgeted as if in embarrassment. Her feigned distress appeared to work because Mary, without saying a word, flung open a walnut chest, pulling out a beautifully-tailored turquoise silk dress. She held it up against Megan.

'This will do. Annie, see to her. If the back is too broad, fix it so that it may be worn and use some extra pins and things to control that mass of hair! Be quick about it the two of you. I shall expect you by the half hour.'

Having given her latest orders, she left them in her room. Annie looked at the mess Megan was in.

'We'd better work fast, Megan, or she'll have you for dessert!'

The two women smiled at each other.

'Is she as bad as her bite, Annie?' Megan asked as she removed her outer clothes and Annie brought her the pitcher of water.

'For a maid, you wear fine undergarments,' Annie said suspiciously. 'And, yes, she is every bit as bad as her bite, so take care, lass.'

She was at least ten years older than

Megan, and very competent at arranging hair. She wasted no time in brushing and fixing Megan's.

'The undergarments were a present from . . . '

'Don't tell me, an admirer?' Annie interrupted and her eyes broadened and her eyebrows raised as she looked in the mirror at Megan's reflection.

What's one more lie, Megan thought. So, blushing because she was partly shamed on the inference, she nodded.

'Well, when Mr Timothy has seen you in this,' Annie said, turning to pick up the dress from the bed where Mary had left it, 'you'll have another one, for sure.'

'I doubt it. I think he's quite taken by Lady Mary.'

'Ha, don't you believe it, girl! He'll not go for mutton when there is lamb to be had!'

Annie laughed and helped Megan into the dress. It was not a perfect fit but, with a small tuck in each side at the back, it fitted her snugly.

'You may not have as broad a back, lass, but you've got more to fill it up front. Now you best get down there, or you'll 'ave us both in bother.'

She held the door open and bobbed a curtsey to Megan in fun as she walked past. Megan laughed and turned to the top of the stairs. Annie returned hastily by the kitchen stairs to help cook. Lady Mary was most particular about everything, including meals.

Samuel was just approaching from the other side. He also had been dressing and wore a fine white cravat that he was having difficulty fastening correctly. He called across the stairs to her.

'Megan, where's Annie?'

He was agitated, she could tell. She walked across to him.

'She has returned to the kitchen to help cook. May I help you?'

She instinctively reached up and straightened the cravat for him, so it hung correctly.

'There, that's better.'

He blushed slightly and she was touched by his humility until she followed his eye-line and realised he was admiring her figure in a way that was too intimate for her liking. When she stepped back to a respectable distance from him, she saw humour in his eyes. However, when he saw Timothy Spencer-Hughes step into the hallway talking to his mother, his smile dropped.

Megan wondered what Mister Samuel Jarvis had to hide from a revenue man. Whatever it was, and wherever it was, she strongly suspected the weasel, Fetcher, had something to do with it.

'You look delightful, miss,' Spencer-Hughes commented. As Mr Samuel joined Hughes at the foot of the stairs, Megan reflected how these two handsome men were as totally different in their mannerisms as in their looks. One was well groomed and full of flattery, obviously a ladies' man, the other brusque with little time for frippery.

'Thank you, sir. Please call me Megan.'

She looked quickly to Lady Mary and was expecting to see, at the very least, a curt look of disapproval, but was surprised to see the opposite was the case. Lady Mary stepped next to her son, leaving Megan to be walked into dinner by their uninvited guest.

'You are quite the most beautiful young lady I have seen since arriving here, Megan.'

He leaned over as if whispering a secret between the two of them.

'And how long have you been here, Mr Spencer-Hughes?' Megan asked inquisitively.

'One week.'

'Then you will not have seen many to compare, sir,' Megan replied quickly.

She was not easily taken in by compliments. To Megan, they were only appreciated if sincere. She doubted his were. He eyed everyone and everything he saw as if taking an inventory.

'You are too modest. Please call me Timothy.'

Samuel opened the dining-room doors to reveal walls of maritime blue, surrounded by a white and aqua border. The oblong dining table was laid with a white cloth edged with Venetian lace. It was laid with silverware on it and like the crystal glasses, they sparkled as the fire burned in a deep grate.

Megan thought the dining-room was charming. She was seated opposite the Italian marble mantelpiece on which stood a number of Chinese vases. Samuel Jarvis sat Timothy opposite her with his back to the fire then took his seat at the head of the table after Lady Mary was seated on the chair facing him.

The first course was served immediately.

'Tell me, Mr Hughes, what business brings you here?' Samuel asked.

Megan noticed that the shortening of Timothy's name seemed to annoy him and wondered if Samuel had done it deliberately. She had no love for the Customs services. Megan respected the fact that the government needed to raise money to fight the wars with France, but like her father before her, she suspected they were as guilty as the smugglers of profiteering from the extortionately high prices. Either way, it was not sensible to rile the Customs service.

'Unfortunately we have reason to believe that there have been smuggling activities in these parts.'

'Good heavens!' Mary exclaimed. 'I thought that sort of thing was stamped out years ago when George Walton was arrested and imprisoned.'

'Indeed, ma'am, it was. The previous owner of this manor headed a truly brutal gang of rogues and we smashed them. However, the discovery of Jack Atkins' body has rekindled the belief that activities have started again.'

'Gracious!' Mary uttered in disbelief.

'Have you arrested anybody?' she asked and looked as if she were hanging on to his every word.

'No, ma'am, not yet.'

He glanced at Samuel who seemed more interested in his food, until he spoke.

'I understand Jack's body was found washed up on the beach near Stangcliffe. Why should that equate to smuggling activity?' Samuel asked, looking directly at Timothy.

'We have had reports of sightings of a lugger anchored offshore on the night he went missing,' Timothy replied.

'He was a good lad. His father worked the land for years. Jack was not your smuggling type,' Samuel said dismissively.

'Really? What would you consider a smuggling type, Samuel, when our own gentry have been arrested for dealing with contraband?'

Samuel's and Timothy's eyes locked on each other.

'I just meant he struck me as an honest, simple lad,' Samuel replied and focused his attention back on to his meal.

'If he was, why did he have a black neck scarf in his pocket?'

'Perhaps he meant to wear it,' Mary offered.

Timothy grinned at her.

'My dear lady, precisely. However, they use them to wrap around their faces so as not to stand out in the dark when contraband is landed and unloaded. He could very possibly have been one of their tubmen.'

'Oh,' was all Mary said innocently.

Megan thought of the black cloth under Fetcher's bed, and looked at Samuel in a different light. Then she noticed the oil painting above the fireplace opposite. A face looked back blankly, that of a well-dressed gentleman with a grand wig. He stood proudly with one hand on a globe of the world. Behind him was the sea and the distinctive painting of a large ship.

He obviously was a successful man. Something troubled her about him. The face was familiar, but the colouring fairer.

'Are you admiring my late husband, Megan?'

Mary's voice provided the answer to her unasked question. He was Samuel's father.

'Yes, milady. He looked a fine man.'

Something troubled her, though. It was not until the end of the meal when she could have a closer look that she realised what it was. The ship was a slaver. Megan despised the man instantly, the money and the household under whose roof she now slept. The blood of innocence had paid for all this!

She had listened to William Wilberforce speak in person at a rally. One day soon the trade must cease, but that day would not come soon enough. So tempted was she to lead Timothy Spencer-Hughes straight to Fetcher, incriminating Samuel Jarvis in the process, but commonsense prevailed. She had no desire to be found at the bottom of a cold, heartless cliff, like Jack Atkins.

5

Life at Monkton Manor soon fell into a regular pattern of a normal manor house existence. Lady Mary gave absolute instructions that she was never to be disturbed before late morning. Megan gladly obliged and was fond of rising early.

In a short time she had made herself familiar with the manor and the other servants. Annie was friendly with Harriet Barton, the daughter of the inn, so it was with some delight that early one morning, as they sipped warm milk together in Megan's room, she was able to tell Megan the tragic circumstances of Jack Atkins' death.

'Well, Megs, the word is that he had been out that night as a lookout, but was unfamiliar with the coast, being a country lad, and had been blown clear off the headland by the strong gale. A tragedy for his doting mother, who apparently is so bereft, she can only blame foul play. She's so full of grief, Harriet tells me, that she's all but isolated herself from the other people in Seaham.'

'What does her husband say?'

'Nought! He's dead, Megs. That's what's made it so bad. Jack was her bread and butter. If Mr Samuel wants to, he can turf her out of the fisherman's cottage. She'll never pay her own way, now as she's gone quite mad. I think he'll have her put away like.'

'Oh, no! He can't.'

Megan thought of the horror of the asylums where those who are ill in the mind were thrown mercilessly with those who just couldn't cope with life. Once there, they stood little or no hope of ever getting out.

'He could if he wanted to,' Annie said gravely, as she collected their two glasses and stood up.

'No doubt.'

Megan thought of the inhumane ways in which slaves were stacked like cargo into ships, side by side, head to toe, men, women and children. Anyone who could reap profit from that with a clear conscience would not flinch at the thought of a woman being placed in an asylum, particularly if that same woman was making accusations near Mr Timothy Spencer-Hughes, threatening a smuggling operation. She would not go to the authority, but Megan decided she would help the woman. But how could she?

'Annie, can you ask Mr Fetcher to saddle my horse? I wish to take a ride before milady awakes.'

Megan peered across the landing to Mary's bedchamber but, as the door opened, she ducked back inside her room. She heard Mary's door close and looked out to see Fetcher's back descending the servants' stairs! Whatever was the hired hand doing in her mistress's bedchamber?

Megan leaned against the wall of her

room, letting the realisation sink in. Perhaps Mary was not a true lady after all? What would Mister Samuel think of her? He was out making his fortune bigger, no doubt, whilst his servant was being familiar with his mother.

Megan dressed quickly for riding and made her way to the stable yard. As she appeared, so did Fetcher with a horse.

'Have you milady's permission to go out riding?'

His question and manner were blunt as she mounted the beautiful hunter. She guessed correctly — he had saddled a spirited animal for her. Their dislike of each other was mutually apparent. Was he jealous of the barrier her presence placed between him and access to Lady Mary? Perhaps Samuel was not such a blind fool after all. He may not care, so long as all appeared respectable.

'My lady sleeps. I shall return before she rises.'

He let go of the horse's reins.

'Do,' he said, then slapped the horse's rump.

It burst into a gallop heading straight for the bridge that crossed the small river. If Megan had not been a competent horsewoman she would have ended up head first in the river. Instead, she let it have its head as it galloped along the drive. By the time she reached the manor's gates and the open road she had the animal well under control.

Fetcher had in fact done her a favour. She needed a fast horse to take her to Seaham and back, leaving her enough time to visit the bereaved Mrs Atkins. Megan didn't know why she felt the desire to see her, or what she would say to the woman once there, but her instinct told her to go. She could not stand by and have an innocent woman tossed on to the streets, or worse, thrown into a madhouse.

She rode straight to the small group of fishermen's cottages that nestled behind the inn. Most of the town's folk were out going about their business. Instead of taking the open coach road, she followed the narrower path that went through the wooded ravine, bypassing the hamlet. Before she could see the open bay, Megan smelled the fresh, salty sea air, and heard the gulls that perpetually flew round the headland of Stangcliffe.

From thick woods, she suddenly found herself almost behind the inn itself. Perfect, Megan thought, for hiding contraband. If Timothy found or knew about this track he would have the perfect place for an ambush. She stopped for a moment to watch a group of children playing on one of the two-wheeled trolleys that were used to haul the cobles over the sand and breakers, and into the sea.

Megan tethered the horse to a cart at the side of the end cottage and walked up to the door, knocking twice. The other women she could see were busy collecting cockles and mussels from beneath the cliffs. The door opened wide and Megan lifted her head to speak, but instead of a feeble, defenceless, mad woman, Samuel's figure, as tall, proud and handsome as ever, stood before her. Suddenly she was at a loss for words.

'What is wrong?'

Samuel looked as confused by her sudden appearance as Megan was at his. Her mind was reeling. He obviously thought she had come to see him.

'I came to offer my condolences to Mrs Atkins, Mr Samuel.'

She lifted her chin up as if standing for her right to be there when she was far from certain she had any right at all.

'Did you? Well, I'll pass them on. Now return.'

He glanced around and saw the horse.

'Return to the manor and your duties, taking extremely good care of Trojan as you go.'

'Trojan?'

She glanced down at his hound that was standing at his side. It slept in the stables but was always present as soon as Samuel left the house.

'This is Finn.'

Samuel pointed an angry finger at her horse.

'That is Trojan and you have no business riding him or leaving expensive blood stock tied up like a cart horse!'

The colour was flushing his cheeks. Megan turned to go then, despite herself, she spun back around to face Samuel.

'I merely wanted to know if she needed anything.'

'And what position are you in to give her help, should she need it?'

Samuel's words were sharp but his colour was subsiding slightly as a half smile crossed his face. To Megan, he was mocking her. If only he hadn't been there she could have passed the woman some coin to see her through.

'I did not want to see a helpless, grieving woman thrown on to the streets or worse, because she could not pay her rent!' she snapped out.

'You would stop this, would you?' Samuel said in a quiet voice that seemed to be filled with a threatening, cold fury.

'If I could, yes,' Megan answered but had taken a step backwards.

She thought she saw a pale face in the window but when she looked again it had vanished.

'Go back to your mistress whilst you still have a position to go back to!'

Megan was seething. No-one had ever dismissed her like that. She turned to retaliate but he slammed the door shut as he re-entered the cottage. Duly dismissed, she mounted Trojan and walked him back along the track. Megan was in no hurry to return to the manor.

Angry thoughts filled her head. Samuel Jarvis stirred her emotions in many strange ways. She was surprised when a rider came up the track at speed behind her. Megan turned to find Samuel Jarvis glowering at her as they turned into the drive of Monkton Manor as the track joined the new coach road.

'Does my mother know you are out here?' he snapped.

'No, she sleeps still,' Megan answered without hesitation. 'Fetcher saddled this horse for me. I did not request your hunter.'

He looked ahead thoughtfully for a few moments.

'You ride him well, but do not take him out again. He is very valuable. I shall speak to Fetcher.'

'How is Mrs Atkins?' Megan asked.

'Mrs Atkins?'

Samuel looked at her as if he had been distracted from some deeper business.

'What is she to you?' he asked absently as if not comprehending her compassion for a woman she did not even know.

'She is a woman without means, who is also a woman grieving for a child. She is very vulnerable,' Megan replied, adamant that she would fight this woman's corner.

'Really, and are you a champion for women in distress, or a busybody?'

Her eyes flashed with rage and curls cascaded by her cheeks as she quickly turned her head to face him. He laughed openly and mockingly.

'She leaves on Thursday morning.'

'You're having her evicted?'

'To Newcastle, yes.'

Samuel was looking at her, in total amusement. She wanted to hit him, strike his arrogant face, knocking the patronising manner out of him.

'To an asylum?'

Her head was reeling. How could he? How could anyone be so heartless?

'What a lovely image you hold of me, dear Megan.'

He brought his face close to hers.

'To her sister's. She is not safe here. She makes wild accusations.'

Without warning, he cupped a hand behind her head and kissed her lips, then turned his horse to face the drive and kicked it on.

Megan stayed for a minute, letting all the hot-headed sensations settle in her veins. The hatred, the anger, the exhilaration, the warmth, the disgust and the longing were all tearing at her mind. She could never let herself fall under the womanising skills of a slaver, no matter how handsome and confident he was. She rode back to the manor and was glad to have to rush to her room in time to change and see to her mistress.

Soon she would be free but not when Mr Timothy Spencer-Hughes was still suspicious of everyone around Seaham. She may have to bide her time until Mr Samuel overstepped his confidence and Timothy smashed his smuggling ring.

However, she would never snitch on them, not even on the creature, Fetcher. They weren't the hard men of Cornish wreckers, but she had no doubt that the retribution of such men would be vile. Samuel was right to give Mrs Atkins a safe passage out of the hamlet. If not, she might find herself joined with her beloved son.

That night a gale blew up followed by slicing, cold rain. The storm started in the early hours and Megan lay awake in bed listening to the squall. She hoped the following morning when they went to church, as they did each Sunday in Seaham, that she would be able to stay awake throughout her uncle's sermon, which would be long and dated.

The next morning was sunny, cold and calm. Their coach drew up outside the church and her aunt greeted them. Megan had been polite to her since their first meeting but had not indulged in any conversation with her. There was as strong a chill between them as there was in the air.

Fetcher coughed as he jumped down from the front of the coach. Samuel and Mary both looked back at him as he almost doubled up with the exertion on landing.

'Have you caught a chill, man?' Mary asked.

'Yes, ma'am,' he said honestly, and with no air of familiarity.

When Mr Samuel was there he was always distant with Lady Mary. Megan could see that Timothy Spencer-Hughes was walking to meet them with another man in uniform.

'Then go and find somewhere warm to sit, man. We cannot have you barking like that in church.'

Mary looked at Megan's aunt.

'Goodness, we would never hear the good Reverend speak. Be along with you.'

Fetcher ducked behind the coach and was out of sight before Timothy was upon them. Megan thought she saw Fetcher slip down the alley to the inn. He must have been the lookout last night, Megan thought, as she remembered the storm. Foolish man, Megan thought.

'Timothy, how nice to see you.'

Lady Mary was in her element being the perfect, pious, caring lady before all gathered. She looked from Timothy to his companion, obviously waiting for her introduction. It duly came.

'My Lady Mary Jarvis, Mr Samuel Jarvis, please welcome Captain Spencer-Hughes of the Dragoons stationed beyond Gorebeck, my brother.'

Megan watched as Mary's eyes lit up and Samuel's seem to glaze over, especially as Mary had duly invited them for dinner. Timothy never seemed to refuse any invitation given. Mary seemed keen to matchmake, and was increasingly encouraging Megan to sit, read, play music or eat with Timothy. Handsome he was, exciting and exhilarating he wasn't.

She glanced at Samuel, but before her thoughts took her any further along memories of his kiss, Mary shouted over to Harriet Barton. Samuel almost flinched. It was obvious to Megan that he knew she wanted him, but Harriet was as common as her mother but better, if not tastefully groomed.

She arrived in a vision of a garish green co-ordinated hat and dress. A modest shawl was wrapped around her shoulders. She had been huddled quite tightly in it, until she approached Samuel, then it slipped slightly off her shoulder. She had too much make-up on but still she held her hair and head high.

'Harriet, dear child. Are you well?' Mary asked the unsuspecting girl, who was obviously flattered at being called over to their group.

Some of the fishing wives stopped before entering the church as if witnessing Harriet's dream come true. Was she going in with the gentry? Harriet's head seemed to rise farther into the air as she answered Mary.

'Yes, milady.'

She turned and looked up as coyly as she could manage.

'Mr Samuel.'

He nodded in acknowledgement of her and looked away.

'Harriet, this is Mr Timothy Spencer-Hughes who works for the Customs service and his brother, Captain

Spencer-Hughes of the Dragoons, stationed at Gorebeck.'

Harriet positively preened at them.

'Glad to meet you, sirs.'

They also nodded politely, but Megan could see the mockery in their eyes.

'Now, please be good enough to find Mr Fetcher for us and tell him to send word to the manor this instant that we are having two guests for dinner.'

Mary's smile was sweet but the look in Harriet's eyes hardened as she realised she was not being invited to join the group to even up the men and women.

'Why, of course, Lady Mary, if I only knew where he was then I would gladly go but the service is about to start.'

Mary wasted no time.

'Oh, yes, of course, but that is why I called you. He will no doubt be in your father's inn, girl. Be quick and you'll make the service. Be sure to give him the message, or I'll hold you responsible.'

Megan felt a tinge of pity for Harriet as the girl duly nodded and walked off, head bowed. She had been dismissed as the innkeeper's daughter.

'Come, gentlemen, we must not be late for the service.'

Mary walked ahead with the Spencer-Hughes and Megan was left to walk into church alongside Samuel. Her mind was a whirl of thoughts and emotions about the man sitting next to her, when her uncle took the pulpit and waited for everyone's attention. Megan contemplated the chances of him saying anything that would take her out of her current confused state over what to do about the situation at the manor when her uncle's words cut through her like a knife.

'I have this morning some very good news and, indeed, some very sad news. I have been informed that we have won a great battle, Trafalgar. We can rejoice, for God has given us a great victory over the enemy at sea.'

The church rippled enthusiastically,

rumours of an end to war with France. But then her uncle continued.

'However, my children, the brave Lord Horatio Nelson did his duty and lost his life. We have lost a great man, and it is with this sad loss in mind that we have a service today, not of pure jubilation, but to remember those who have died.'

The congregation sat in stunned silence. Samuel looked solemnly down at his hands on his lap. He was gripping them until his knuckles were almost white, as if struggling to control his emotions. He looked at Megan for one split second, as he must have sensed her watching him. She thought his eyes looked moist. He seemed touched by what he obviously thought was her concern and so, without saying a word, squeezed her hand before standing to sing the first hymn.

6

The mood over dinner was sombre in the extreme. The usual small talk had been replaced by long silences. The men spoke in tribute to the memory of Lord Nelson. Samuel looked grave, and a great sadness seemed to have befallen him.

Megan stared absently at the stone angels carved into the surround of the fireplace. Their eyes were tilted heavenward as they held on to throngs of carved foliage. Mary seemed agitated, as she tried to stimulate a conversation.

'So, gentlemen, have you captured the ruffians?'

Mary addressed her questions to the two brothers. Although Megan could see similarity around their eyes, they were very different in stature. The Captain was shorter and slighter in build, and, Megan guessed, a few years older.

'I fear not, but we will and soon, Lady Mary,' Timothy answered as he smiled across the table at Megan.

She averted her eyes to her plate, preferring he would let his eyes drool at the contemplation of eating rather than watching her. His attentions were becoming more persistent and Mary did not seem to miss an opportunity to bring them together. Was she trying to rid herself of Megan's shadow, so that she could spend more time with Fetcher? Megan cringed at the thought.

'I like a man to be confident,' Mary gushed.

'We have reason to. Our intelligence in the area is most promising and reliable,' Timothy answered in confidence.

His brother watched Samuel, whose face remained impassive.

'My brother informs me that this manor was in fact the centre of the notorious gang of smugglers led by George Walton.'

'That was before we moved here,' Samuel said. 'This is a working farm and manor house. We have no need of such things. What we don't provide for ourselves we can buy in York.'

'I'm pleased to hear it,' Captain Spencer-Hughes replied. 'Are you a man of independent means?'

Samuel's colour was starting to rise, but quelled to his mother's timely intervention.

'Captain, my dear, late husband was a successful businessman. He owned ships in Bristol, London and Hull,' Lady Mary said proudly. 'That is his portrait, gentlemen, above the mantelpiece.'

'Oh, I see.'

Both men admired the fine portrait of an obviously affluent man.

Slave ports, Megan thought, and instinctively flashed a look of pure hatred towards Samuel. Their eyes met as he had been watching her also. For one second she thought she saw a puzzled, hurt expression in his.

'Tell me, Timothy, where are you staying?' Mary asked, determined to keep the conversation going.

'I shall be moving into the old cottage on the headland tomorrow. It has been under repair, and has excellent views of both the coast and the sea. A beacon lit there can summon the dragoons in very little time.'

The two brothers smiled smugly at each other.

'We shall soon clean up this small hamlet and move on.'

'To bigger and better fish?' Mary said with glee and raised her glass as if in salute to the promising future they would be assured if they claimed a victory for HM Customs. 'I thought that old Nell's cottage was supposed to be haunted?' Mary continued in a concerned manner. 'She was accused of witchcraft, some thirty or forty years since. I remember my maid telling me the tale. The locals won't go near to it.'

'How very convenient for the smugglers,' Timothy answered dryly and they both laughed.

Megan ate quietly and was thinking about having seen her uncle and Samuel huddled in the corner of the vestry after the service, deep in conversation. When Mary had sent her to find him when it was time to leave he had seemed ill at ease and had stopped his conversation instantly. Was her uncle in league with Fetcher? It was obvious to Megan. They had a church and a hall, both of which were well-known places for hiding and dispensing contraband. The fools!

'Miss?' the captain said to Megan. 'You seem lost in thought. Is something wrong?'

Megan flushed and felt unsure what to say. Honesty was not the best policy here, of that she was sure.

'No, sir, I mean — yes, I was.'

'Good heavens, girl, what do you mean?' Mary snapped at her.

'May we share them, Megan?' Timothy asked casually but sat looking at her as if she were going to divulge some useful piece of information to him that would help his quest.

'I was thinking of all the lives that were lost along with Lord Nelson's.'

'True!' the Captain reflected. 'We should remember all our sailors who died so bravely in the battle.'

'Well, yes,' Megan continued and had had her fill of patronising looks and small talk. 'Not only ours. I mean if the French lost thousands of men, too, then I feel sorry for all the families and bereaved on all sides of the war. War is a terrible thing.'

The two men looked at her as if at a loss as to how to reprimand her, for Megan could see that is what they would like to do. She did not look to Samuel.

'Well, we could feel sorry for all the rats and cats as well but we should not get carried away, dear child!'

Mary's voice was light and mocking,

but it turned an embarrassing silence into a congenial moment of humour at Megan's expense, making her feel like a naïve and innocent child.

'You have made a valid point, Megan. Where death is concerned, people grieve on all sides, no matter the political or moral rights of the war.'

Samuel's voice was calm and she gave a quick nod of appreciation for him supporting her comment. At least she finished the dinner without feeling completely unworldly.

After they left, Mary headed straight up to her room after telling Megan she did not require her. She was too bereft by the news and wanted nothing more than to retire with her thoughts for a great man. Samuel was about to call Megan when he hesitated. They both heard a cough coming from the library.

Without turning, Samuel shouted, 'Fetcher!'

The surly face of Fetcher appeared around the doorway. He walked into the hall.

'What are you doing in here, man?'

Samuel's voice was harsh. Megan stepped into the drawing-room. Fetcher hated her enough without her being present if he were to be reprimanded. Besides, didn't Samuel know how much time Fetcher spent in the house when he was out on the land?

'I was . . .'

Fetcher seemed to be at a loss for words, Megan thought. Usually he moved around the house almost unobserved but his cough was loud and intrusive. He was heard everywhere.

'If you want something for that cough, see cook. If you are cold in the stable, sleep by the kitchen fire, but stay out of my library!'

Samuel's order was firm. Megan could hear the man's cough become more distant as he left. Then she heard Samuel's voice.

'Megan, come into the library.'

Megan followed Samuel into a room lined with books. He sat down in a yew chair at one side of the fire and watched her enter.

'Close the doors, Megan.'

She followed each order without question as much out of curiosity as obedience.

'Sit down,' he said and gestured to the empty chair, then as an afterthought added, 'please.'

Megan sat and folded her hands together on her lap, then looked up into his face. He still looked pale. Ever since he had heard of Lord Nelson's death, he had seemed visibly shaken.

'Megan, I want to ask you some questions and I want you to answer me honestly.'

He was staring intensely at her.

'I will, if I know the answers.'

Megan was bemused, puzzled as to what he was going to ask her, in such a sombre manner.

'Have you heard any rumours amongst the servants regarding Jack's death?' he asked without taking his eyes off her.

'No, only that he may have been

122

involved as a lookout.'

Megan thought for a moment.

'But everyone knows as much is possible.'

She watched Samuel's face but he gave away no trace of his feelings. Was he frightened of being caught? He seemed too cocksure of himself, she thought, for that to be true.

'Do you suspect anyone's involvement here at the manor?'

Megan stared back at him, looking straight into his eyes. So that was it. He wanted her to be foolish enough to confront him. Why? So he could deny it, or worse, pass the blame to her uncle?

'No, Mister Samuel, I have no reason to suspect anyone. Then I am recently new to this household.'

'I'm aware of how long you have been here. That is why I am asking you. You share no loyalties with the other servants and have a fresh eye. You may see as odd what others take for granted. Also, Miss Clegg,' he paused as he said her real name, 'you may have more of an eye for such things than most.'

'Whatever do you mean by that remark?'

Megan could feel her hackles rising. Whenever her father's name was used in anything but respect she defended him to the hilt. She had done since she was a child. Other children sometimes teased her because of his nickname, Mad Jack Clegg, but she knew how to fight her corner. There was nothing mad about him. He'd been daring, courageous, quick-witted and loving.

'I mean your uncle confided in me of your father's more colourful business dealings. It was bothering his conscience that I had Mad Jack Clegg's daughter under my roof with my lady mother and was not aware of her parentage!'

His voice was angry but controlled as he spoke in low tones.

'Did he, indeed?'

She stood up with her hands clenched in fists by her side.

'Did he tell you that never has he been arrested or tried for anything?'

'Yes.'

Samuel looked at her, his face softening slightly.

'Please, sit down, Megan. I am not going to turn you out. You have a temper that you need to learn to control.'

Megan opened her mouth to speak, but he put his hand up.

'Don't say anything you will regret later.'

She sat down again, in silence.

'So you have seen nothing?' he asked, his voice gentler.

'Nothing!'

'Why did you cast me such a dire look in the dining-room? Did our fathers know each other?'

'I have no idea, Mr Samuel. I've explained I was distracted as I was thinking perhaps we should rejoice a little at the end of the war with France.'

Megan was surprised by his question

but reasoned he must be thinking she suspected him.

'The end. This is but the battle of the sea, Megan. All hell will reign on land now. The war will change but it will continue. It can not do any other.'

Megan listened and was devastated by his words. Surely, she told herself, he must be wrong.

'Once the war is fought on land it will last years. Then, should we win on land, too, the celebration will be short-lived.'

He was standing now, leaning with arms outstretched against the mantel-piece staring into the empty fire grate.

'Men will come home to find jobs have been taken by machines, steam-powered machines. No, our future, Megan, and the hamlet's, is far from secure.'

Although part of her was touched by his obvious sincerity she could not avoid answering his outcry.

'You are rich. Your father secured his family's future with his trade.'

She snapped the last word out with more venom than she meant to. He turned and something in his face showed almost a tinge of humour.

'Is that what galled you? We are rich? It cannot be.'

He studied her face and she looked away. His hand cupped her chin and turned her head to face his. She could feel his breath on her lips as he spoke softly to her.

'You hate the trade, don't you?'

Megan felt she would burst with the indignation of his humiliating and patronising ways. She pulled herself free before he could attempt to place another kiss on her lips. How dare he presume! Yet inside her as she looked into his eyes she felt a deep and sinful longing. Something about this man attracted her.

'Oh, Megan, you are against slavery, are you not?'

Megan had no time to answer, as there was a knock on the door. Samuel stepped back to a respectable distance from her immediately.

Annie opened it.

'Begging your pardon, sir, but Lady Mary is asking for Megan.'

'Very well,' he said. 'Go, Megan, and do your duty.'

Megan left and was glad that at least he knew her true feelings about the slave trade. If she had to leave, she would be glad to. But before entering Lady Mary's room, she took a moment to breathe deeply and resume her normal composure. Try as she might she could not dismiss the feel of him holding her face, or the passion with which he had spoken of the daunting image he had for the future.

7

Lady Mary had Megan read to her from the Bible for a short time then sent Annie to fetch her some warm milk.

'I feel I'm coming down with a fever, Megan. My spirits are so reduced by such sad news about Lord Nelson. Leave me and do not disturb me in the morning.'

Megan left and retired to her own chamber. She tried to sleep but could not. Her mind and body were in complete confusion as to what emotions she was really feeling. Samuel's face crept in behind her lids, and she could not rid herself of her thoughts of him. He was attractive and, after listening to the passion of his words, a man of some vision, but she could not condone his heritage of spilled blood. Megan would never allow herself to feel anything for such a person.

Then there was Timothy Spencer-Hughes. He was well educated, handsome in a way, and always attentive, yet she did not trust him. His eyes took in everything, but his mouth was full of small talk that told her very little about the true man. At least with Samuel he was direct, blunt even.

With only a few hours' sleep behind her Megan rose early the next morning, dressed and packed her things into her bag. She had made a decision. No matter what Lady Mary felt like this morning, Megan would see her briefly to tell her she was leaving. She could not possibly stay at the manor a moment longer than necessary. Mr Samuel would have to give her the agreed allowance which he held for her, and she would make her way to York.

She placed in her pocket her letter of introduction to Messrs Spent and Ashcroft, which her father had given her in the event of his death, with strict instructions not to present it until one year had passed by. She would just have to arrive there some months earlier. Hopefully, Timothy Spencer-Hughes would not follow her. She needed to access her father's money from his other business, without arousing the Customs authority's suspicions. Megan left her bedchamber and crossed the landing to Mary's door.

There was no answer to her knock. Megan decided she must be asleep, so quietly she entered the dark room and approached Lady Mary's bed. Megan was surprised to find it had not been slept in. Where was she? She opened one of the heavy drapes slightly to let in some light. Lady Mary's boots and riding outfit were missing. Quickly and quietly Megan ran down the staircase to the kitchen, and then across to the stables.

As she approached Fetcher's room, she heard a stifled groaning noise. Megan picked up a crop as she passed by one of the stables and looked up at the stairs she had once climbed, but it was not up to them where her eyes settled, but through the stairs. Huddled together, exhausted, were Mary and Fetcher. Both looked exhausted. Mary was cradling Fetcher, as she held him, half in and half out of what appeared to be the entrance to a tunnel.

'Help me, girl!'

Mary's voice was not so much sharp as desperate. Megan put down the crop and, between the two women, they pulled Fetcher into the stables. Mary closed the trap door to the tunnel. She then moved a stool and some tack and Fetcher's tools, leaving no trace of any access, just a stable wall.

Megan looked down at the grey face of Fetcher who, although he was wet, seemed to have an extra moisture to his skin which was coming from within. The two women worked together to help Fetcher to the yard. They needed to get him into the warmth of a fire and a bed. The faint clip-clop of a horse on the drive, approaching the manor, could be heard as they emerged from the stable block.

'Quickly!'

They half-walked him, half-carried his light frame across the yard to the kitchens. Annie saw them and ran over to help.

'Megan, go to the front of the manor and greet whoever it is,' Lady Mary ordered.

'It's Mr Timothy Spencer-Hughes, the revenue man. I saw him from the window,' Annie said excitedly.

'Annie, you help me get Fetcher to my room,' Mary snapped.

'I'll distract him, as long as I can.'

Megan took herself through the kitchens, into the hall to open the main door just in time to see Timothy ride up with his great coat fastened tightly against the cold.

'Timothy,' Megan said with enthusiasm and a broad smile.

'Megan, what a lovely welcome.'

He dismounted and walked over to her, kissing her hand tenderly as he returned her greeting.

'You must be cold. Will you take breakfast, as you visit so early?'

Megan walked him into the entrance, meaning to take him straight into the old hall, but Samuel was already up and dressed and stood staring straight at Megan.

'Timothy, what brings you back here so early on a day such as this?'

Megan looked at Samuel's face. He seemed angry with her. Was it because of the previous night? Did he object to her familiarity with Timothy, inviting him into his home? Did he already know about Fetcher? Whatever the reasons, Megan had to stay calm.

'I need to talk to you, Mr Jarvis, about some activities around Stangcliffe last night.'

Samuel turned to Megan.

'Have Fetcher see to Timothy's horse and have Mary bring up a tray for him.'

Then he turned to Timothy.

'Come into the library. We can talk there.'

Megan excused herself and walked back to the kitchen. So he did not know about Fetcher, Megan thought. She told cook about the requested breakfast tray as she crossed to the servants' stairs.

'I don't know what this place is coming to. Used to be I'd get notice of people's comings and goings. Now it's we need this, we needs that.

Cook shook her head as she disappeared into the dairy room. Megan quickly ran around to take Timothy's horse into the stable block, then ran up to her mistress's chamber.

'Annie, cook's doing a tray for Mr Timothy. Can you take it to the library as soon as it's ready?' Megan asked her friend.

Lady Mary had changed into some dry clothes and was frantically brushing out her own hair. Fetcher's boots and wet clothes were bundled together on the floor and he lay wrapped up in a warm blanket on the bed. He still looked pale. Mary must indeed love him, Megan thought, but it was soon proved wrong.

'What happened?' she asked.

Mary did not look at all surprised by her question. The current situation dismissed their ranks, as she was obviously indebted to Megan and in need of her help.

'He was out last night, but he did not realise, the fool, that Timothy was using the old cottage. Everyone, including Fetcher, believed the place was haunted. Fetcher even claimed he'd seen old Nell, and wild horses wouldn't drag him back there. He feared no-one who still lived, but ghosts were different. They terrified him. I tried to warn them before he could lead them back to us but I found him in the tunnel. He'd collapsed. I left him there and continued to the inn. Amos knows all about Timothy's and his brother's plans. He'll get word to the tubmen and the villagers. They may get the lugger but they'll not catch anyone on land.'

Mary finished brushing her hair and

put on a respectable lace cap.

'Come with me. We shall see what business Mr Timothy has at this hour of the day. Then I'll send Samuel to get that wretch some help. He needs medicine.'

The two ladies entered the library with a calm air about them as if all in the world was sweet and perfectly normal.

'Mother!'

Samuel stood and seemed to struggle with the surprise of seeing her up and dressed so early.

'We have an early guest this morning.'

'So I see. If I'd known you would return so soon, Timothy, I would have had a bed made up for you, then you could have stayed the night,' Lady Mary said as she sat down on the chair Samuel had vacated.

'I was informing Samuel of increased activity last night. The revenue cutter gave chase to a lugger laden with goods.'

Mary leaned forwards in anticipation.

'Did you catch the blackguards?' Mary asked.

'No, alas, but we are now certain that Seaham is in the midst of this trade. If anyone offers you a cheap supply of brandy, tea, tobacco, silk or chocolate, ma'am, you are duty bound to inform us at once,' Timothy said earnestly.

'I shall indeed, and I shall inform cook she must let me know if anyone approaches her, too.'

Lady Mary looked Timothy straight in the eye as she spoke. Megan could not help thinking that they were two of a kind but Mary was extremely talented at deception.

'So for your own safety, ma'am, my brother will arrive later this day with some of his dragoons. They will stay on this estate while we swoop tonight and crack this ring once and for all.'

Samuel rounded.

'Would it not be proper for you to seek permission from me first? You, sir, presume too much on my hospitality.

This is a working manor farm. I do not want it crawling with soldiers.'

Megan watched the two men square up to each other. They were as different as dark and light, good and bad, but Megan was confused as to who was good.

'I don't think you realise this is a matter of national security. There could be espionage afoot. Secrets or agents can be traded just as well as goods. Would you stand in the way of us defending our nation, at a time when the great Lord Nelson has given his life in the same cause?'

Timothy stood looking pious and self-righteous in the extreme.

'Of course not,' Samuel began but instantly Mary was on her feet and looping her arm in Timothy's as she pointed him towards the door.

'Then let us agree on it. Please ask your brother's men to respect our property and animals as Samuel has worked so tirelessly to return this estate to its full potential.'

Timothy looked at Samuel.

'Of course we will. Good day, sir.'

'Megan,' Mary said then paused for a moment, 'have Timothy's horse brought to the front of the manor.'

It was a young lad who walked Timothy's horse around. Timothy did not see anything odd about this but Samuel looked at the boy and then at Megan. He obviously hadn't a clue what was going on. As Timothy rode his horse down the drive, Samuel turned to Megan.

'Where's Fetcher?'

Megan looked back at Lady Mary, who smiled sweetly at him and said simply, 'Samuel, I fear he's not well. Perhaps we could discuss the matter inside. I feel one of my headaches coming on, exposed to this intolerably cold air. Really, I wish you'd consider moving back to London, dear.'

She led the way back into the manor with an increasingly irate-looking Samuel behind her. Megan was amazed that for someone who had such clear foresight about the possible future of the world, Samuel would appear to be blind to what was happening under his own roof.

Megan followed them in.

8

Samuel stood next to the walnut, long-case clock by the doorway of the library. He shut the door behind him and turned to face the two women.

'What is going on here?' he demanded to know.

He was staring directly at Megan and deeply-accusing eyes locked on her as his mother sat down on the yew chair by the fire.

'It would appear Fetcher's heart has let him down. He needs to see a doctor, Samuel.'

Mary's voice was calm and controlled.

'Could you ride over to Gorebeck and ask Dr Bevin to come immediately, dear, before those horrid soldiers arrive?'

Lady Mary shuddered her shoulders as if to emphasise her point.

Slowly he turned his gaze to his mother, who was casually arranging her skirts around her legs as she sat.

'Have him moved into the house whilst I go for the doctor then I want some straight answers from you,' Samuel replied impatiently, as his gaze once again settled firmly on Megan.

'Fetcher is in the house, Samuel,' Mary responded unabashed.

'Where? I will see him before I go.'

Samuel walked towards the large, oak door.

'In my bed, dear.'

Mary's voice remained calm, as she raised her eyes to focus on her son. Megan watched her calm demeanour and could not help admire the sheer nerve of the woman.

'What!'

Samuel looked at his mother, obviously confused and annoyed by the events that were unfolding.

'Well, Samuel, he collapsed on the kitchen staircase. It was merely the nearest bed to place him in. It made perfect sense to me. I could hardly have him laid out on the kitchen table.'

She looked at him straight in the eye, then turned casually to Megan.

'Mind you, I'll not sleep in those sheets again, girl.'

Megan watched as the lady lied through her teeth and did not hesitate or flinch, not even when lying to her only son. Who, Megan thought, could ever trust such a cold-hearted woman as this?

'Samuel,' Mary implored, 'he looks very ill dear, so hurry.'

'I'll go and see him for myself,' Samuel said, as he stormed out of the room.

Megan watched the doors close behind him in stunned silence. She realised for the first time that he had no idea about the smuggling. He was so busy overseeing the estate that he had been blind to the goings on of Fetcher and his mother at the manor. Yet, he had been so opposed to Timothy's and the captain of the dragoons' presence. Why?

Samuel flew out of the library in a blind rage. He climbed the stairs three at a time and entered his mother's bedchamber. The figure huddled on the bed in front of him looked fragile and wan. At first Samuel thought he was already dead, but as he walked towards him, Fetcher's eyes opened.

'What happened to you, Fetcher?' Samuel asked, trying not to feel repulsed by the figure lying on his own mother's bed.

For a long time he had suspected that this man was involved in the local smuggling ring. He had to find out as much as he could before the dragoons arrived. Samuel had no love for the preventative forces. He abhorred the severe taxes that were crippling the ordinary people, but he would never stoop to smuggling. Samuel would not let everything he had worked for be dragged through the mud, especially not his mother's reputation.

'I will go for the doctor, Fetcher, but

first I must know what happened.'

The man half closed his eyes, as if focussing all his attention on answering his master.

'I collapsed in the tunnel. She helped me up here.'

'The tunnel exists?'

Samuel watched as the man, who could hardly breathe, managed a smile. He wondered if the miserable wretch thought of him as a complete and utter fool.

'She?' Samuel asked thinking only of one, Megan, the smuggler's daughter.

The Jezebel pretended to be so naïve, so proper and so caring about the plight of slaves. He had brought her into his own home and had been so cruelly betrayed by her wanton greed. She had brought this trouble to his home, after all the hard work he had put into it, turning a rundown estate with a tainted past into a respected, self-sufficient working farm. Much worse, she risked ruining the reputation of his mother. That, he would not tolerate, no matter how attractive he found her.

Fetcher lay there, still trying to find the strength to speak.

'Did Megan help you up here?'

Samuel leaned over him, and as he already knew he would, he heard Fetcher breathe a raspy, 'Yes.'

'Rest, now,' Samuel said, still feeling a chill in the pit of his stomach at the deathly look of the man.

Samuel ran down the stairs to the kitchen and across the courtyard to the stable block. He walked quickly around each stable, looking for any obvious signs of the tunnel he had foolishly believed was no more than a fisherman's tale. Now he knew it existed, he prayed that the dragoons did not. For sure, he would make Miss Megan Clegg reveal its secrets on his return, then she could help him seal it up for ever.

He saddled and mounted his best hunter and made for the open road to fetch Dr Bevin from Gorebeck. So irate was he that he had allowed such a creature, beautiful as she was, into his home and became so close to both he and his mother, that he did not see the soldier on the ridge who was following him.

Megan and Mary sat for a few minutes, expecting Samuel to re-enter the room. It soon became apparent he would not when they heard him galloping his horse off down the drive. They looked at each other in silence.

'Why did you not tell him the truth?' Megan asked as Mary moved to the long window so she could watch her son leave.

She had dispensed with the formalities of titles. Lady Mary was a smuggler, a thief and had no more entitlement morally to be referred to as a lady than Megan herself.

'Why?' Mary repeated mockingly. 'Because, child, he would never believe it of me. Like his father before him, he only sees me as a woman, a mother, a wife, not a person with a brain of my own.'

Lady Mary gazed out of the window.

'Perhaps you underestimate him.'

Mary's head shot round and she glared at her as if Megan had spoken with audacity.

'Perhaps he does not doubt that you have a brain, but would never think of your character lending itself to masterminding a smuggling ring behind his back.'

Megan stared defiantly at her as she spoke. Megan could see the hurt and anger in Mary's eyes. How many years had she sat like a bird in a gilded cage, resenting it and longing for something to quench the need for adventure, Megan wondered.

'Careful, girl, you have no room to cast aspersions. My husband knew your father when he lived in Bristol. They did business together also.'

Megan flushed. Her father would never have traded with slavers, surely not. She was appalled by the thought and wanted to lash out at this self-righteous woman in indignation.

'Fetcher, he is your friend, is he not?'

Megan asked pointedly, trying to control her temper.

'Friend?'

Mary took her eyes off the window for a moment and looked at Megan and then almost doubled up with laughter.

'Girl, I don't know whether to scold you for suggesting such a foul creature could be my friend or embrace you for making me laugh at such a ludicrous idea. You have a lot to learn about this world. People use people all the time.'

Megan glared at her. Even if Mary were correct, she had never used anybody and would not willingly use anyone.

'Either way, your aspersions are completely and hopelessly wrong. The man is no more than that of a partner in crime, a man with the local knowledge and contacts to do the deeds, whilst I visit York and use my social circle to supply affluent buyers. It is very convenient for us both. However, I do feel the blackguard is becoming too familiar and taking too many liberties. I've no doubt he brought all this about by his clumsy disposal of Jack Atkins.'

'He murdered the boy?' Megan asked in disbelief.

How Lady Mary could stand there and say such things without any sign of remorse appalled her. Mary gave a quick glance in her direction and then chuckled.

'My, we are naïve.'

Something caught Mary's attention outside.

'We are busy today. It appears we have another visitor.'

'The dragoons?' Megan asked, nervous that they had arrived so soon and without Samuel being there.

'No, girl,' Mary chuckled. 'Your dear uncle on an old nag, which looks like an overgrown donkey.'

Mary's laughter was interrupted when a distraught-looking Annie flung open the door.

'What is it, girl?' Lady Mary asked.

'It's Fetcher, milady. He's dead!'

151

Mary fidgeted nervously, obviously distressed.

Mary walked over to the door, shouting orders out as she did so.

'Annie, come with me. Megan, tell cook to prepare tea for you and the good Reverend in the old hall, then keep him there as long as you can. Tell him that I am ill with remorse for the loss of Lord Nelson. I've been sickly and distressed ever since the news broke. Samuel is very concerned for my health and has gone for Dr Bevin.'

Then they heard a frantic knock at the door.

'Move!'

Mary's command was not needed as both women were already carrying out her instructions. By the time Megan returned from the kitchens, Lady Mary was nowhere to be seen.

'Uncle!'

Megan sounded genuinely surprised as she opened the door and saw her uncle, looking cold, wet and obviously very disturbed about something.

'I must speak to Master Samuel urgently. Something awful has happened.'

'Uncle, please come in.'

She took him straight to the warm fireside in the old hall.

'Mister Samuel is out. He has gone for Dr Bevin.'

'Why? Is Lady Mary ill?' Reverend Tully asked with a sincerity that touched Megan.

In fact, Megan was so taken by the distress of her uncle that she momentarily lost track of what she was supposed to say and could only think of the truth.

'Megan!' the Reverend's voice snapped, bringing her out of her thoughts.

'Yes, Uncle, she is. Nothing too serious, we hope. We think she's been taken aback by Lord Nelson's death. It has hit her hard, like so many. A national disaster on the back of victory.'

Megan felt ill at ease lying, especially to a man of the church.

'Tell me what's happened.'

'Oh, Megan, I thought I could help her. I tried so hard. I even asked Mr Jarvis to talk to her himself. He did but she was intent on vengeance. Master Samuel tried to get her out of Seaham. She knew what was occurring, who was doing what. She should have gone, but she wanted vengeance.'

'Who was?' Megan asked, not understanding to whom he was referring.

'Betty Atkins, Jack's mum.'

Her uncle twisted his hands together in agitation.

'If she'd just gone and left it to us it would have been all right. But, no, she had to go to the lookout cottage the night before she was due to leave. She had no faith in me or God.'

Reverend Tully looked up at her, cradling his warm cup in his hands.

'I suppose you have no reason to either?'

Megan averted her eyes.

'I do believe in God, but I don't understand all that is allowed to happen in the world, Uncle, like war.'

'But you have had no reason to believe in me,' he added, but Megan stayed silent. 'I thought so. My welcome to you was not as Christian as it should have been, but trouble has been brewing here over the previous months. Then with Mr Timothy Spencer-Hughes arriving, followed by his ambitious brother, they started asking questions. The last thing Seaham needed was the arrival of the daughter of Mad Jack Clegg. They might put the whole thing on a much grander scale than it was, linking up unconnected groups around the coast. That is why Master Samuel said he would take you into the manor. We never suspected that we were taking you into the thick of it. I've never liked that man, Fetcher. I'd never have credited him with the brains to run the whole show though. When George Walton was arrested, Fetcher had an alibi over on Beckton Moor. He was cleared.'

Megan sat amazed. Her uncle had

been trying to protect her, not disown her!

'So what happened to Betty Atkins?'

'She was seen. I suspect it was Fetcher.'

He lowered his voice as he spoke. Megan wanted to tell him it was too late, the man was already facing his final judgement. She could not, though. To do so would make him a party to the goings on at the manor and she did not wish to compromise his position.

He continued, 'She was found this morning. She'd been beaten to her death as a warning to others not to betray them and their despicable trade.'

Her uncle looked silently into the fire.

There was another knock on the door, which was followed by a loud pounding and then the hall doors were opened wide by Captain Spencer-Hughes with six dragoons behind him.

'What is the meaning of this?' Reverend Tully demanded.

The Captain looked undeterred,

Megan thought, although he may have preferred not to see Reverend Tully sitting there.

'We're here to search the house!'

He signalled to his men to go through the rooms of the house. He himself headed upstairs.

'You can not do this! Milady Mary's abed,' Megan shouted as loud as she could, hoping that Annie's sensitive ears could hear her warning.

Reverend Tully stood up to protest but a dragoon forced him to sit down.

'Never have I known such outrageous behaviour. You will stop this fiasco now!' her uncle retaliated, but to no avail.

'I can and I will. This household is suspected of harbouring contraband and I am to find it!'

Captain Spencer stormed up the stairs taking two men with him. The Reverend turned to Megan.

'He aims to be promoted, but this I fear will be his undoing!'

Megan looked at her uncle. She

prayed he was right, but what of Fetcher's body? If it was found in Lady Mary's room, what explanation could be given? And how much about the goings on at the manor did they already know? Megan could only sit with her uncle and wait to find out.

9

Samuel entered his home and was instantly greeted by the sight of armed dragoons in his entrance hall.

'What is the meaning of this?' he demanded to know. 'Who is in charge here?'

Before he received an answer he heard the sound of a woman's scream.

'Mother!' he yelled and ran up the stairs to her bedchamber, with Dr Bevin following on behind him.

Lady Mary's door was wide open and Captain Spencer-Hughes was standing trying to apologise to a distraught Lady Mary.

'What is the meaning of this?' Samuel repeated his question.

Two dragoons left the room. They had obviously been rummaging through drawers and the oak chest.

'We are searching for contraband. We

have reason to believe that this manor has been the centre of the smuggling ring again, and you, sir, have been implicated.'

The Captain, red faced, rounded on Samuel.

'What? How dare you!'

Dr Bevin rushed over to Lady Mary.

'My dear lady,' he said to her gently and she whimpered pitifully in reply.

'How dare you enter here! This woman has a high fever and is delirious. You, sir, have acted like a barbarian. You are a disgrace to your uniform! Your superiors shall hear from me.'

Dr Bevin's outrage mirrored Samuel's but his words as he looked at his mother lying spent in her bed, stunned him. She was sweating profusely and looked very weak.

'I shall continue the search, and will leave once I have found the contraband,' the Captain said as calmly as he could but the threats from both a priest and a doctor were obviously unnerving him.

He had to find something or, as Megan and everyone else knew, the ramifications of his actions would not sit well with his superiors.

'You will leave this room, now!' Samuel ordered.

This time, the Captain did as requested and called his soldiers from the bedchambers.

'Found anything?'

The soldiers shook their heads in reply. Annoyed, he pushed past them and returned to the entrance hall, where his other men were waiting for him.

'Anything?' he bellowed at them.

'No, sir.'

'Your superiors will hear of this invasion of my property, Captain.'

Samuel stood before him. Megan and her uncle were in the doorway of the old hall.

'I shall send a full report of what I have witnessed here today to the Bishop,' Reverend Tully said and stood firm by Samuel as Megan made her way to the stairs.

'There are still the outbuildings to search.'

Timothy's voice surprised them as he strolled out of the library.

Megan stopped on the stairs and looked down on him.

'You would do this to a home that has made you welcome on many an occasion?'

'Dear Megan, we do our duty. We take the risks, we catch our thieves and we get our rewards,' he said smugly.

'In this case, I feel, Mr Hughes, you shall get your just rewards.'

The Reverend's voice was calm and directed at the Captain, whose neck and face were now flushed red. He looked, Megan thought, a worried man. But what if they still found the tunnel?

'You shall all wait in the old hall until the search is complete.'

The Captain left two of his men guarding the oak doors.

'I will go to Lady Mary,' Megan said.

'You will do as you are told. She is

with her doctor. There is nothing more to be done for her.'

Timothy's voice was sharp. Samuel took a step forward but was blocked by a dragoon. They could do nothing but wait.

When Timothy returned, he, too, had patches of red on his cheeks.

'It would appear we have been misinformed on this occasion. However, the man, Fetcher, is nowhere to be found. We would like to question him. Where is he?' he asked as if justifying their behaviour by the absence of their main suspect.

'At this precise moment, I have no idea as I have been kept a prisoner in my own home by a group of ruffians in uniform,' Samuel said.

'Samuel, you should understand we had to do this for your own good, to clear your name from any malicious gossip,' Timothy said in a tone which was now filled with platitude, his old smooth manner having returned.

'Excuse me, I have an ailing mother

to see to. You will leave my home and never, ever return. I shall send my complaint directly to both your brother's and your superiors forthwith.'

'Samuel,' Timothy began to speak but Samuel brushed past him.

Megan followed closely behind. Even the Reverend ignored his attempt at an apology by holding open the door for him to leave with his shamefaced brother and the dragoons.

When Samuel entered his mother's room he heard Annie's relieved voice say, 'It's all right, milady, they're all leaving.'

'Thank goodness for that. I thought I would expire with the heat.'

Mary removed the bed covers, revealing she was fully dressed under her shawl. Annie scooped up a bedwarmer wrapped in a sheet. Megan watched the amazed look on Samuel's face as his mother wrapped a blanket around herself and casually sat on the chaise. She was obviously hot but not in anyway ill. Dr Bevin sat on the end of the chaise.

'Well, Mr Samuel,' he said, 'it would appear your mother will make a full and speedy recovery, but where is the real patient?'

Fortunately, Megan thought, he was a friend of the family. Samuel looked at Megan.

'Well?'

She shrugged her shoulders as she had no idea where the man's body had been hidden and looked at Mary.

'Under the bed, wrapped in blankets,' she answered whilst adjusting the material covering her legs.

'He has managed to stay exceedingly quiet for a man who could not easily catch his breath,' the doctor said, as he looked under the bed.

'He died,' Megan said, 'just before the Reverend arrived. Then he was followed shortly afterwards by the arrival of the dragoons.'

'We could not think what to do, Samuel, so we hid him and, as he was lying in my bed, I took the patient's place,' Mary explained. 'It was the obvious thing to do.'

She looked helplessly at her son. The two men looked at each other.

'Does the Reverend know of this?' the doctor asked.

'No,' Megan replied, 'he has no idea. Uncle believes the lady is ill with remorse over the horrific loss of Lord Nelson.'

'Just as well. Samuel, I think you will need my help here,' Dr Bevin said.

'Megan, go down to your uncle and tell him I shall speak to him when I have calmed my mother.'

Samuel gave her the order. There was no softness in his voice at all. He sounded harsh. Megan supposed he was shocked by the happenings at the manor and upset by his mother's part in it all.

As soon as Megan descended the stairs her concerned uncle met her.

'Is the good lady all right?'

'Yes, Uncle, she will be fine, just a little frustrated by the shocking intrusion of her home.'

Megan felt herself fill with guilt. Lying did not come easily to her.

'Praise the Lord for that. I shall be writing to the Bishop. Those two will be in for a dressing-down. They treat the villagers the same way. I had better return to your aunt. If they have searched the vicarage or defiled the church in any way she, too, will be distraught. It is all the doing of that man, Fetcher. I found out as much from Harriet Barton. He's been using the manor as his cover, but he runs the whole thing. Funny, I never gave him credit enough to be the brains behind it. He'll be halfway to London or somewhere by now with all his illicit gains, I should imagine.'

He sighed and looked relieved that he had at least made peace with his niece.

'Why did Harriet tell you this?' Megan asked her uncle, thinking that in view of what had happened to Betty Atkins she would be the last person to say anything.

'Because her father was implicated, as owner of the inn. Apparently they searched it from top to bottom but found no trace of any hidden goods. They only found what they thought was a tunnel, but it turned out to be an old mining works that was empty and led nowhere. She came to warn me they were heading for the manor. Her father sent her to me.'

He put his arm around Megan's shoulders as he walked to the door.

'Is Amos part of it?' Megan asked her uncle, whom she now knew had no ties in the trade at all.

'Of course, but he's clever, Megan. Nobody can prove the obvious. However, he is a marked man and will have to stop for he will be watched. Seaham will now have a regular patrol. I'd best return. Please give my regards to your mistress and Master Samuel.'

With that he patted her cheek gently and climbed up on his old horse.

'You must visit with us. It is time we got to know our niece and stopped overlaying the sins of her father on her.'

He smiled at her and left. Annie was returning to the kitchen when Megan closed the doors.

'Annie, what's to be done?' Megan asked.

Mary whispered to her, 'It's already in hand,' then continued about her business.

'Megan!'

Lady Mary's voice echoed down the stairway.

'Yes,' Megan answered as she entered the room looking cautiously around her.

'Do you expect to see a ghost, girl? Where are your manners? What happened to addressing me properly, respectfully?' Mary asked.

'I lost the respect. You lie, you steal and you are totally unmoved by murder. What are you?'

Mary laughed in her face.

'I'm a lady, and that, child, you will never be.'

'If that is what it takes to be a lady

then I am glad I will never be one!'

Megan turned away from her to leave.

'I did not dismiss you,' Mary said sternly.

'No, you did not need to. I am dismissing myself. I am leaving.'

Megan did not look back but thought she heard Mary laughing.

Megan carried her bag down to the kitchen.

'Wherever are you going, Megs?' Annie asked.

'I am going to stay with my uncle tonight and shall leave tomorrow on the stage to York.'

Megan pulled her gloves on.

'Without waiting for Mr Samuel to return? He'll be livid,' Annie reprimanded her friend.

Before Megan could answer, Samuel's figure appeared behind Mary.

'He already is! Come with me!'

He stormed back out into the yard and crossed to the stable block, expecting Megan to obey him without question. She followed him in, thinking he was reluctantly saddling a horse for her to return to the vicarage. As soon as she entered the stables he rounded on her.

'Where is it?'

The fury in his voice unnerved her, and angered her at the same time. He was facing her and he was obviously very angry.

'Where is what?' Megan asked, not understanding what he was inferring by his question.

'The tunnel. It exists and you knew it existed. I suspected your uncle, God forgive me, of planting you here, but he is innocent. It is you, Miss Clegg, who are guilty. You and Fetcher between you have nearly destroyed my household.'

Megan's colour rose.

'How dare you talk to me like that! Yes, I know where the tunnel is because I helped Fetcher out of it. He had collapsed and was stuck half in, half out.'

'Where?'

Samuel leaned over her. She felt his breath on her cheeks. Pushing him away, she went to the open stairs where she had piled tack and saddles up as if stored behind the stairs.

'Behind there. You have to push there firmly and it releases the whole panel from a hidden catch. Then it opens like a door. It is quite ingenious, because if you press anywhere else it does not move.'

Megan watched, as he did not move anything but studied the top of the panel.

'What is in there?' he asked without looking at her.

'A tunnel,' Megan answered, not meaning to be sarcastic but honest.

She did not know and did not want to know what was in there. She hated tunnels.

'What have you stashed in there and where does it come out?'

Megan's mouth opened in disbelief. Did he honestly think she was working with them? It obviously still had not penetrated his thoughts that his mother was the brain and Fetcher and his friends were merely the brawn. She turned and walked away, picking up her bag as she went.

Before she entered the yard, he spun her around by her arm and held her firm. She looked back into his familiar ebony eyes; her face flushed as a whole wave of emotions welled up inside her. How could she love and hate a man in equal parts? She had no doubt that the feelings within her contained a deep longing for Mr Samuel Jarvis, ever since he had stolen that first kiss from her lips.

'You cannot walk away from this. You've compromised my mother, nearly destroyed my home and for what, profit?'

His face was nearly touching hers.

'I don't want your money. Keep what you've made. That's between you and your conscience, but for my mother's and my own safety you must answer my questions.'

His eyes changed their focus and despite himself he kissed her firmly on her lips once more. As her arms relaxed, she dropped her bag. It landed heavily against her leg bringing her to her senses. She pushed him away.

'What do you take me for?' Megan snapped as she collected her bag and strode out into the yard.

He followed her.

'Perhaps I should not have done that, but don't deny you wanted it as much as I.'

Samuel was watching for her response. Megan looked at him silently. There was no point in answering him. They both knew the truth of that at least. She started walking to the start of the long drive in front of the manor, which would in turn lead her to the Seaham road.

'It's a long walk back to your uncle's. Answer me and I'll lend you a horse,' he offered.

Megan stormed back over to him, pausing only momentarily to brush a wayward curl out of her mouth.

'I'll give you your answer, but, Samuel, it is not one you will want to hear!'

His eyebrow raised slightly at the use of his Christian name.

'I don't know where the tunnel goes. I don't know what is in it. I don't care, because I do not need it. When I helped your mother pull Fetcher out of it, I stumbled across them by chance.'

He opened his mouth to protest when she mentioned his mother. She raised her finger to his lips. Samuel brushed it gently aside.

'No, you said your piece, now it is my turn to say mine. You are a blind fool. You have an intelligent, devious mother who has been the mastermind of the revival of the smuggling activities between the town and the manor, and you never suspected her at all, not even when she is capable of hiding a dead man beneath her own bed!'

Megan cringed slightly as if the thought alone gave her a chill.

'That is your answer, and the truth, and I will not stay here a moment longer. Goodbye!'

Without a further word, she set off down the long drive. By the time she was halfway along it, she felt exhausted. Megan would have liked to have at least reached the gates before she rested but she could not. Her energy and temper were spent. She placed her bag on the verge and sat on top of it, removing her bonnet and wiping her forehead on her sleeve. Instantly, a few more curls broke free but she cared not. The faint clip, clop of a horse gathered momentum, until she looked up into the autumnal sun to see Samuel sitting astride a hunter. He had another horse saddled walking behind him as he held the reins in his hand.

'I told you it was a long drive,' he repeated casually.

'Have you come to evict me?' she asked, looking at the spare horse.

'No, to apologise to you.'

Of all the things she thought he

might say, that was not one of them.

'I behaved badly. I am sorry. I have neither been a gentleman or a fair man. I have acted as a judge when I have not had all the facts before me. I am the Master of Monkton Manor and have not even known what was occurring under my own roof.'

He paused slightly, hesitantly, ill at ease.

'Will you accept my abject apology?'

He smiled at her nervously and something inside responded. She wanted to shout, 'Yes!' Instead she said it quietly. He slipped down from his horse and, still holding the reins, embraced her. He brushed her curls with the back of his hand and kissed her tenderly.

'Come back with me.'

His voice sounded as warm as his breath against her cheek.

'I can't. I will not be a servant to you or your mother. I cannot.'

She tried to turn away but he would not let her go.

'You do not have to be, Megan. Don't you see, I want you to be my mistress.'

Her reaction was so quick he had no time to defend himself. She slapped his cheek so hard it left a red mark where she struck him.

'You spoiled, pompous brat of a man. How dare you even think I would.'

'You hot-headed, little fool. I am the Master of Monkton and I want you to be the Mistress of Monkton. I'm asking you to marry me.'

Megan froze; her heart leaped. She could not believe what she was hearing, but then there were her principles at stake. She could not look at him as tears filled her eyes. She turned away.

'I cannot marry you. Your father — his money.'

Samuel stood in front of her. He let loose the reins.

'What has my father to do with anything? He is dead, as well you know.'

'The trade, blood money. I could never agree with it.'

With moist eyes she looked up at him.

'If it were not for that, would you want to?'

He held her close, pre-empting her reply. Megan nodded.

'Then, dear Megan, you are a bigger fool than I. My father and I parted without speaking for fifteen years. I could never accept his callous attitude towards profiting from trading in slaves. However, many people have used the goods from those involved in slavery and profited from it, like your own father did. We can only hope slavery will soon be abolished. I support that, Megan. Let us judge each other for who we are, and not what our fathers were before us.'

Megan nodded agreement.

'Will you be my mistress, then?' he asked.

'Where is Fetcher?'

She heard him sigh, as she had not answered his question.

'Deep in the marsh. He will be

assumed a runaway suspect. Hopefully they will waste many a cold hour searching for him.'

'Your mother will not be pleased at the prospect of our union. Can you ever trust her again, Samuel?'

'After this, she would not dare do anything so foolish again. So say you will marry me.'

'Yes,' she replied, smiling radiantly. 'I will.'

THE END

We do hope that you have enjoyed reading this large print book.

Did you know that all of our titles are available for purchase?

We publish a wide range of high quality large print books including:
**Romances, Mysteries, Classics
General Fiction
Non Fiction and Westerns**

Special interest titles available in large print are:
**The Little Oxford Dictionary
Music Book, Song Book
Hymn Book, Service Book**

Also available from us courtesy of Oxford University Press:
**Young Readers' Dictionary
(large print edition)
Young Readers' Thesaurus
(large print edition)**

For further information or a free brochure, please contact us at:
**Ulverscroft Large Print Books Ltd.,
The Green, Bradgate Road, Anstey,
Leicester, LE7 7FU, England.
Tel:** (00 44) **0116 236 4325**
Fax: (00 44) **0116 234 0205**

CONVALESCENT HEART

Lynne Collins

They called Romily the Snow Queen, but once she had been all fire and passion, kindled into loving by a man's kiss and sure it would last a lifetime. She still believed it would, for her. It had lasted only a few months for the man who had stormed into her heart. After Greg, how could she trust any man again? So was it likely that surgeon Jake Conway could pierce the icy armour that the lovely ward sister had wrapped about her emotions?

TOO MANY LOVES

Juliet Gray

Justin Caldwell, a famous personality of stage and screen, was blessed with good looks and charm that few women could resist. Stacy was a newcomer to England and she was not impressed by the handsome stranger; she thought him arrogant, ill-mannered and detestable. By the time that Justin desired to begin again on a new footing it was much too late to redeem himself in her eyes, for there had been too many loves in his life.

MYSTERY AT MELBECK

Gillian Kaye

Meg Bowering goes to Melbeck House in the Yorkshire Dales to nurse the rich, elderly Mrs Peacock. She likes her patient and is immediately attracted to Mrs Peacock's nephew and heir, Geoffrey, who farms nearby. But Geoffrey is a gambling man and Meg could never have foreseen the dreadful chain of events which follow. Throughout her ordeal, she is helped by the local vicar, Andrew Sheratt, and she soon discovers where her heart really lies.

HOLMES, Valerie
The master of Monkton
Manor

FICTION